ON THE JOB
PERIL, HUMOUR, HEARTBREAK, JUSTICE...NO TWO POLICE SHIFTS ARE THE SAME.

SANDI WALLACE

CONTENTS

Praise for Sandi Wallace's books	v
Also by Sandi Wallace	ix
The Job I	1
Busted	3
The Job II	24
Impact	25
The Job III	48
Hot Patrol	51
The Job IV	60
Losing Heidi	61
The Job V	82
Silk Versus Sierra	83
The Job VI	104
Who Killed Carly Telford?	107
Preview of Tell Me Why	117
Dear Reader	135
More of Sandi Wallace's Short Crime Stories	137
Acknowledgments	139
About the Author	141

Copyright (C) 2017 Sandi Wallace

Layout design and Copyright (C) 2020 by Next Chapter

Published 2020 by Gumshoe – A Next Chapter Imprint

Edited by Fading Street Services

Cover art by Cover Mint

This book is a work of fiction. Names, characters, places, and incidents are the product of the author's imagination or are used fictitiously. Any resemblance to actual events, locales, or persons, living or dead, is purely coincidental.

All rights reserved. No part of this book may be reproduced or transmitted in any form or by any means, electronic or mechanical, including photocopying, recording, or by any information storage and retrieval system, without the author's permission.

PRAISE FOR SANDI WALLACE'S BOOKS

'A beautifully written police procedural, where the characters are every bit as important as the plot. *Black Cloud* brilliantly captures the impact of small-town tragedy, as investigators struggle to cope even as they work towards solving an horrendous crime.'

— **CHRIS HAMMER, WINNER OF THE UK CWA NEW BLOOD DAGGER AWARD FOR** *SCRUBLANDS*

'Aussie Noir at its best. Once again Wallace has tapped into the rural crime genre with an iconic sense of place beneath a black cloud of menace and intrigue. Her Georgie Harvey and John Franklin series just gets better and better.'

— **B. MICHAEL RADBURN, AUTHOR OF THE** *TAYLOR BRIDGES* **SERIES**

'*Black Cloud* is absorbing and suspenseful, a perfect weekend read for the rural crime fiction lover. Wallace has struck that elusive balance between relatable characters, disturbing crimes and an urgent plot that drives the reader forward.'

— L.J.M. OWEN, AUTHOR OF THE *DR PIMMS* SERIES AND *THE GREAT DIVIDE*

'Sandi Wallace's best yet! Engaging, fast-paced, and full of suspense.'

— KAREN M. DAVIS, FORMER NSW POLICE DETECTIVE AND AUTHOR OF THE *LEXIE ROGERS* SERIES

'A gripping twist on the bushfire threat all Australians live with.'

— JAYE FORD, AWARD-WINNING AUTHOR OF *DARKEST PLACE*

'Suspenseful, exciting, atmospheric rural crime; a riveting debut.'

— MICHAELA LOBB, SISTERS IN CRIME AUSTRALIA

'Worthy debut.'

— *HERALD SUN*

'The police aspect of this novel has depth and believability…this debut is a cracker.'

— J.M. PEACE, SERVING QLD POLICE OFFICER AND AUTHOR OF AWARD-WINNING *A TIME TO RUN*

'Sharply crafted and authentic… These are stories that linger, long after they are read.'

— ISOBEL BLACKTHORN, REVIEWER, EDUCATOR, NOVELIST, POET

'Sandi Wallace packs as much punch into her short crime stories as she does into her novels.'

— ELAINE RAPHAEL, GOODREADS READER

ALSO BY SANDI WALLACE

Georgie Harvey and John Franklin series

Tell Me Why
Dead Again
Into the Fog
Black Cloud

Short story collections

On the Job
Murder in the Midst

Award-winning short stories

'Sweet Baby Dies' *(Scarlet Stiletto: The Eleventh Cut – 2019)*
'Fire on the Hill' *(Scarlet Stiletto: The Tenth Cut – 2018)*
'Busted' *(Scarlet Stiletto: The Eighth Cut – 2016)*
'Ball and Chain' *(Scarlet Stiletto: The Sixth Cut – 2014)*
'Silk Versus Sierra' *(Scarlet Stiletto: The Fifth Cut – 2013)*

Non-fiction

Writing the Dream (contributing author)

To the authors who ignited my life-long love of mystery stories and my dream of being a crime writer.

And to the men and women in blue who are ordinary, yet also extraordinary, people.

THE JOB I

I do it for them…for you
because I can make a difference
keep the peace
make it safe
dig out the truth
put troublemakers away
I do it for me, too
because it could lead anywhere
uniform, plain clothes, the brass
on the beat, a squad, covert ops, training, leading
I put myself out there
first response
facing danger
might not make it home
because it's more than just a job

BUSTED

Winner Scarlet Stiletto Awards 2016
Best Romantic Suspense Prize

First published in *Scarlet Stiletto: The Eighth Cut – 2016*

BUSTED

4.00am was Nessa Reid's favourite time to exercise. But since detecting a pattern in people's response to her sharing this—cringing before they inched away from her, their expressions saying she must be insane because nobody in their right mind chooses exercise over bed, especially when it was dark—she decided to keep it to herself.

Admittedly, she had to force the habit for the first few months. After that, it grew on her to the point that now if anything prevented her donning the sneakers and hitting the pavement at that time, she morphed into Nessa-Crankypants-Reid. She got over it if she fitted in an alternative workout, although it never quite measured up. Pre-dawn was the only time she was guaranteed not to have to mediate, pacify, restrain, or sympathise with anyone. For a fleeting while, all she had to listen to were her breaths, foot strikes, and, if she felt inclined, music.

There was a bite to the air today and her breath spiralled in soft clouds as she jogged onto the oval and dropped into push-ups.

She chuckled, thinking gone was the girl who never asked

Does my bum look big? in her navy work pants because the honest answer used to be *No, it looks huge*. These days, she knew her bum drew its share of admiration in her male-dominated workplace or when out with friends. Not that she was in the market for a man. She'd quit them prior to launching her fitness kick.

'Whiff of winter this morning, isn't there?'

Nessa nodded to the speaker, moving into an isometric lunge.

'Bit harder to work out in winter, isn't it?'

She hadn't faced it yet but figured it'd be doable in a beanie and gloves. Nessa swapped legs, sank into a lunge and held it, saying, 'A bit.'

She smiled reflexively, then cursed herself. If she encouraged the guy, he'd break her solitude every time. As it was, she suspected she'd need to change her routine to avoid him. By coincidence or not, he'd jogged up on three out of her last five sessions.

'Great time of day though, isn't it?'

The single floodlight washing over the oval shone on his face as it split into a beam. He scratched his chin. Maybe sweat made his beard itch.

'Yeah, it's great.'

Nessa did a set of squat kicks. The best part of this routine was next on the agenda. She needed to lose the guy.

'Look, er–?'

'Jake.' He grinned and fluttered a wave.

'Nessa.'

'Short for Vanessa?'

Her nose scrunched. She wasn't here for conversation and had always wondered what her otherwise-sane parents had thought naming her *Lanessa*. 'Nope. Anyway, I'm up to my sprint starts. You don't mind?' She gave an apologetic shrug.

'Course not. Happy to join you!'

And bugger it, *he did*, while Nessa feigned a happy face.

A few hours later, she clocked on for her shift, still bothered by the interrupted workout. She pictured the guy —*Jake*—and wished she could run a check on him. She'd met plenty of dubious characters hiding behind beards and she wondered if Jake belonged to that club.

'Nessa!'

She swivelled from her computer to face the senior sarge. 'Yes, boss?'

'Burg.' Sally McCain handed her a note. 'Take Dilly and check it out.'

Nessa's skin tingled. There were burgs and burgs, but coming from Sarge Sally this might be a good one. She'd noticed that the senior sergeant intermittently jumped in over Mac, the desk sergeant, to toss her juicy jobs. She'd never complain about reverse-discrimination, and anyway, Mac himself had given her a wink after she'd closed a tricky case last week and said, 'I can't see you driving the van for too much longer, Reid.'

Was it time to put up her hand for detective training?

Nessa daydreamed about trading the uniform for plain clothes, as she weaved the divvy van through traffic on the highway and turned into a side street. A minute later, she nosed the blue-and-white into a cul-de-sac—if this outer 'burb could claim to have anything that posh—and parked in front of a rendered single-storey home. The property wasn't far from where Nessa lived in a similar-styled house. There was nothing glamorous about the neighbourhood or her place, but it was home and affordable, even after she'd kicked out Mr Wrong. And what wasn't to love about a seven-minute commute to work?

As she and her younger offsider, Nick Dill, started for the front door, a short and stout woman in her sixties ran down the front yard, which was a dense vegie patch split by the driveway and concrete paths.

'At last, you come.'

'Mrs Luisa Occhipinti?'

'*Sì*, of course.'

While Nessa introduced herself and Dilly, she picked up the aromas of garlic and onion, subtle but mouth-watering, that she guessed seeped into the woman's fingers during early lunch preparations. Her stomach growled.

'You hungry.' Mrs Occhipinti smiled and beckoned. 'Come. I have fresh *biscotti*.'

Nessa knew better than to blunder in and disturb the evidence but couldn't stop another embarrassing growl from her gut. She ignored it. 'Could you please give us a little background first, Mrs Occhipinti?'

The woman said, 'No Mrs Occhipinti...*Luisa*. *Sì*, of course, yes.'

Nessa started with, 'Can you tell me about the break-in last night?'

Luisa nodded.

After thirty seconds, Nessa realised she'd have to narrow her questions to get the conversation going. 'How did the offender get in?'

'The back door.'

'Did they force the lock?'

The little Italian woman's face turned into a tomato. 'No, it wasn't locked. I leave it open for my Renatie, cos he's on night shift and that way I don't have to worry about him waking up the whole-a-neighbourhood if he can't find his keys.'

'You were home when the break-in happened?'

Luisa bobbed her head.

Nessa hid her surprise. Home intrusions were rare this side of the city and usually motivated by drugs or personal vendettas, rather than opportunistic theft. She was also stunned by Luisa's calmness – was that because she had nothing or everything to hide?

The older woman cupped her hands together against her cheek. 'Asleep.'

She looked so darned cute that Nessa believed her. 'You'll keep your doors and windows locked from now on, right?'

'*Sì*, of course.'

That, she didn't believe. Luisa sounded just like Nessa's mum when she agreed to do something, then immediately did the opposite. She smiled wryly and asked, 'What time did you discover the theft?'

'Renatie come home about-a-five, like usual. He saw the mess the people make but maybe he's too tired, cos he don't think anything really wrong, just come to bed. I saw it when I got up this morning and called the *polizia* and that was a-long-a-time ago.'

Nessa tried to apologise, but Luisa flapped her hand. 'S'okay. You people very busy.'

Grateful for a nicer-than-average customer, Nessa continued. 'Any damage? Or vandalism?'

'No.'

The lack of violence or damage pointed to simple theft after all. Nessa asked a few more questions, then she and Dilly followed Luisa to the kitchen.

Pots bubbled on the stove, and diced tomatoes and parsley filled a chopping board. Ordered domesticity, except for cupboards and drawers sitting ajar, their contents strewn.

Luisa drew Nessa's eye and shrugged. 'I leave it until you come and see.'

'What was taken?'

'The money from my purse – about-a-hundred dollar. Renatie's old phone but it's no good because it doesn't have a whatsitsname–?'

'SIM card?' Dilly suggested.

'*Sì*, yes. The people do *this*,' Luisa waved her hands, 'but don't take-a-much.'

Little monetary value involved, along with no violence or damage, meant it was too minor to call in the Ds or a crime scene unit. Most other uniforms would've processed and forgotten the case, but Nessa was intrigued. She ignored Dilly's impatient watch checks while Luisa plied them with coffee and almond biscuits, and didn't rush, knowing Sarge Sally had selected her for good reason.

Unfortunately, after leaving the address, other callouts and patrols took priority, right up until Nessa clocked off. She flipped into civilian mode, happy to be on day shift again tomorrow and able to do her 4.00am workout.

A movie and late dinner with girlfriends filled her evening. Despite going to bed not long before midnight, Nessa was already awake when her alarm bleeped, reflecting on the past eight months behind her closed eyelids. She'd chosen to ditch her useless boyfriend but had still been heartbroken, her self-esteem shattered, along with all hope of decent sleep. Eventually, she'd traded frustrated sighs in bed for a chain-smoking walk. The walk became a wheezy jog. Once that turned into a circuit program with running, she'd already shed five kilograms and almost succeeded in quitting the ciggies. She reckoned she had the habit beat after surviving New Year without a smoke and had chipped away at the next five kilos, relieved that her preferred regime coincided with the coolest part of the day over a relentless summer.

Nessa pulled on a tracksuit, covered her sandy-blonde corkscrews with a cap, grabbed keys and a water bottle, then jogged towards the park.

She'd only been there a few minutes when the bearded guy galloped up. Unsurprised, she sighed softly.

'Morning, Nessa!'

She returned the greeting and began her routine, kind of annoyed and yet impressed with Jake's confidence when he shadowed her.

Nessa grinned when she noticed he puffed more than she did during the star jump and push-up suicides. Then again, he was talking all the way through, not seeming to mind that she was less chatty.

'So, what do you do?'

The inevitable tricky question. People reacted one of three ways when she told them she was a cop. They did a runner, mounted their high-horse, or tried to crack onto her – suggesting things involving her handcuffs and pistol. Early on, she decided to massage the truth until she knew the person better.

'Childcare.' It wasn't much of a stretch.

His pupils grew, turning his eyes almost black. 'You like kids, then?'

'Yeah.' Nessa grinned. She adored kids, particularly her niece and two nephews. Their innocence diluted the crap she saw daily and gave meaning to it: to keep them safe. 'And what do you do?'

'Sparky. Mainly commercial electrical.'

Nessa smiled. She liked to spend her time after hours with friends who did normal jobs. Like electricians. She grimaced. Since when did she consider this Jake guy anything other than an interruption?

Later in the morning, with a stab of guilt, Nessa drifted back to that moment in the park. She shouldn't have lied. She loved her job and real friends had to accept it as part of her. And honestly, this Jake could end up being a good mate if she gave him a fair go. He enjoyed pre-dawn workouts, liked kids, barracked for her footy team, and his favourite food was Italian – four big ticks in her book, even if he talked too much during exercise.

Mac, the desk sarge, cut across her thoughts. 'Nessa, can you do us a favour and switch to nights tomorrow? Patto's done his knee and I don't have anyone else.'

They were permanently under-resourced. 'Sure.' She lifted

her palms with a shrug and a smile, pretending she wasn't bummed. Days and afternoons were okay for her 4.00am workouts but the graveyard shift stuffed it up completely.

The remainder of her shift went routinely, and Nessa went home to force her transition to nightshift.

She ate eggs on toast at what should've been dinner time, vacuumed instead of winding down in front of the TV, delayed going to bed by reading what would've been a good book if she weren't so tired, and ignored her body clock at 3.50am promising herself to train that evening before work. She sighed, thinking it was one way to avoid Jake, and turned the page of her novel.

Almost exactly twenty-four hours later she was actually glad that work had stuffed up her routine when a fresh job came in. Break-and-enter while the homeowner slept in bed. Odds-on Luisa's robber had struck again. And with luck, he'd have made a mistake that'd help them nab him.

She mentally corrected herself to *he or she*, chased it with a yawn, then realised that was too hard for her shift-change-lagged mind and thought, *bugger it, just call it 'he' for now*.

She was partnered two-up with Big Phil and he drove, non-negotiable. So, while he zipped through the neighbourhood illuminated by streetlamps and the very occasional house light, Nessa mentally mapped the area.

If she drew compass points from the park where she trained, her own home sat to the east, Luisa's to the west and the latest job to the south. The crook had yet to hit north or east. She decided to remind her elderly neighbours to double-check they'd locked up until they caught him. And they would catch him. Small-scale crooks always made mistakes.

'Next house, Phil.'

Her partner nodded and pulled up the driveway.

Nessa compared the property to Luisa's. Both were detached from their neighbours. Both had side gates left ajar, presumably by the crook. However, this house had been modernised and extended, its garden landscaped.

Minutes later, she discovered that Luisa Occhipinti and Heather Smythe were as different as their homes. Ms Smythe towered over Nessa's 174 cm, almost matching Big Phil's height, and was slim, of Anglo-Saxon descent, and condescending. She gave their boots a pointed glare, sighing loudly when they left them on. Coffee, bickies, and the use of first names weren't offered at this address.

But a victim was a victim, no matter whether the cops liked them or not. So, Nessa and Phil followed protocol.

Consistent with Luisa's break-in, the crook had avoided violence and left most of the place unmolested. He'd broken a lock on the back door and entered while the vic slept. Her alarm hadn't been armed. None of the expensive, bulky electrical equipment had been touched. A smartphone, iPod, stash of cash from a tin in the kitchen, and digital radio were nicked. Smythe's two teenage kids weren't home and there wasn't mention of a significant other, which corresponded with Nessa's guess that Smythe was a divorcee forced to downgrade from a classier district in order to keep her kids in private school – and she'd remind them of that great sacrifice until they were old and wrinkled.

Nessa thought they'd wrapped things up, but Smythe had saved the best for last.

'When I entered the room,' she gestured towards the kitchen, 'he was standing there holding my handbag. I said, "Put it down." And he said, "You shouldn't leave it lying around, lady." Then he emptied out everything.' She pointed to the paraphernalia on the granite top and sniffed. 'He stole my mobile and purse.'

Nessa asked, 'Was he wearing gloves?'

Smythe's lips puckered as she concentrated. 'It was dark except for the beam of his torch and difficult to see. But no, I don't believe so.'

'We'll take your handbag for fingerprints, then.' Nessa bagged the item, adding, 'As you saw and spoke to the offender, we'll need a description.'

Smythe lifted her chin, peering down her nose. 'I drafted a statement for you and sketched him; I'm quite talented.'

It turned out to be a passable statement, which would do for the interim, and a terrible image, but at least they had a starter on their guy. They finished their questions and promised to keep in touch.

'When will the CSI department arrive?'

Phil's mouth quivered, possibly suppressing a rare smile. 'Ma'am, fortunately for you, the scale of this matter doesn't necessitate a visit from our crime scene crew, but rest assured we'll fully investigate your case.'

Smythe did a cockatoo screech. *'What?'*

'You're fortunate there's no damage and the loss is of small monetary value.'

Smythe's cheeks mottled. 'But–'

'You're also lucky that the offender didn't take more – or attack you when you interrupted him.'

Smythe huffed but gave up when Big Phil stared her down.

Back in the van, he hesitated with his hand over the ignition. 'So, what've we got, Reid?'

She summarised: 'Broad, dark-haired, possibly a teenager but could be as old as twenty-eight and a little above my height. He wore a baseball cap with a fluorescent Metabo logo, so Smythe couldn't see much of his face but "he seemed hairy". Blue jeans, black hoodie, sneakers, backpack. That description could fit hundreds of males in the area and plenty on our books.'

'Yeah, not that helpful.'

With that, the big guy turned over the engine and they headed for the station.

Throughout the rest of that shift and the next two nights, they spent any available time working through possible candidates for the home invasions. They interviewed several possibilities, but Nessa's instincts told her they were non-runners.

At the thought of running, she craved her morning workouts and wondered if Jake would still be at it when she finally went back on days.

A few hours before her next night shift, Nessa double-checked security as she left her house and jogged to the park. She debated which of her usual circuits to do. Undecided, she found herself revolving in a circle in the middle of the oval.

She stopped. To her right was home, on the left Luisa's, and behind her lived Snooty Smythe, all approximately a kilometre from here.

Was there a pattern to their crook's work? Would he target one of the other two directions soon? Would he follow the same timeframe?

He'd turned over Smythe's place three mornings after he'd robbed Luisa. They'd had busy shifts the last couple of nights, but there had been no jobs with the same MO. Did that mean their crook would strike again tonight?

Nessa's stomach flipped. She'd lay money on it, but Mac or Sarge Sally would say she didn't have enough, whereas Big Phil would drop one of his dark stares, making it obvious what he thought of young upstarts, particularly those without a dick.

What to do? Take out a patrol car one-up and check the area? What time? Luisa was robbed after midnight—when she'd scoffed a block of chocolate in the kitchen—and before her husband's return at 5.00am. Smythe called in her burg at 4.00am.

How could she convince Phil to let her out alone for those five critical hours?

Matters were taken out of Nessa's hands when her shift started with a nasty car accident, followed by a domestic dispute. While they continued to negotiate with the blueing parties, she heard a call to a nearby hot burg picked up by another car.

Thirty minutes later, they returned to the station, processed the husband, and dumped him in a cell to sober up. Nessa immediately dialled a number.

'Smiley,' she greeted Chele Smilik, her counterpart at the adjacent station. Chele's nickname was both a twist on her surname and a nod to her perpetual good mood, which came in handy for Nessa now.

'How's things?' her friend returned.

They chatted for a few minutes, then Nessa switched to business. 'I heard you handled a burg in our area a couple of hours ago?'

'Yep. Small-scale theft, the only thrill being that the owners were home at the time.'

Nessa contained her excitement. 'What was nicked?'

'Couple of hundred bucks and a few gizmos belonging to the teenage daughter. That's about it.'

Faking laid back, Nessa said, 'I'm guessing side-gate entry, then through the back door, probably forcing the lock?'

'Spot on.'

'No other damage and no violence.'

'How do you do it?' Smiley joked.

'We're seeing a pattern on our patch. But you mentioned the *owners* plural were home?'

'Yep. The hubby and wife were in. Their kid was at a sleepover.'

Nessa mused aloud, 'Our burgs involved women on their own.'

It still seemed more than coincidence.

Smiley chuckled. *'Hubs and wife were having nookie when the break-in happened. Wife was red-faced about only hearing the burg when he broke a vase.'*

Nessa laughed.

'By the time they put on some clothes and went downstairs, he was already on the run.'

Nessa's breath caught. 'They *saw* him though?'

'Yep. Our bloke—if we have a match—is tallish, well-built, and wore jeans, dark windcheater and a cap.'

Nessa hazarded, 'A Metabo cap?'

Smiley rustled in the background. *'Correct. So, we have a match.'*

'Seems so. They only saw him from behind?'

Smiley made a buzzer sound. *'No. The bloke's cap got caught on a shrub and he turned around when he lost it. Both witnesses said he had short, thick, black hair. Hubs said he had a beard and wife reckoned stubble. Gotta love the powers of observation in the general public, don't ya?'*

Nessa chewed her pen. 'Anything else?'

'That's the gist of it.'

About to end the call, she belatedly asked the key question: 'The address?'

When her friend named a court around the corner from Nessa's house, she felt a wave of adrenaline.

They disconnected and Nessa mulled over the cases. She deduced that the crook would strike again in three nights and to the north of the park; the only direction he had yet to hit.

All she had to do now was catch him in the act. She grinned.

At shift changeover, Nessa was finishing a report when Mac approached her desk and rapped his knuckles on the top.

'Shop.'

Nessa smiled wearily, wondering if he had good or bad news. 'Hit me with it, Mac.'

'You're back on days from tomorrow, kiddo. We'll sort out your rest days later. Unless you want to stay on nights, that is?' His laugh rumbled through the quiet muster room. He shook his head. 'I didn't think you were that mad.'

And when her alarm bleeped at 3.50am the following morning, she sprang out of her warm, comfy bed, letting out a laugh that sounded like Mac's. Maybe she *was* mad.

Nessa sprinted to her park, then jogged on the spot, checking her watch. She was a little early.

A couple of laps of the oval later, her stomach knotted with disappointment.

Then a voice from behind said, 'Nessa.'

She spun around, almost colliding with the travel mug Jake thrust towards her. 'Coffee?'

Nessa took a mouthful and savoured the soothing, strong hit. 'Ah, nice.' She smiled. 'You always have a spare with you?'

'No, I saw you arrive and ran home to get one for you.'

Embarrassed when warmth flooded her cheeks, Nessa lifted the mug to take another mouthful.

'Oh shit, I forgot.' Jake dug through his right tracksuit pocket, then the left. He held out a couple of sugar sticks. 'I didn't know if you take sugar and took a guess you'd like it white.'

'This is perfect, thanks.'

Now he blushed through his beard, which she noticed he'd trimmed.

Nessa frowned as she processed a thought. 'You live close, then?'

'Yeah, about a K in that direction.'

North. In the vicinity of where she believed her crook would next hit. She debated whether to retract her lie, admit she was a cop, and warn him to take care with security.

Her gut tightened. What if Jake wasn't as nice as he made out?

She stared at him, unconvinced that he wasn't part of the

dubious bearded-character club. Then she considered the descriptions of the crook from the witnesses. Smythe said he was hairy. The hubby at Smiley's break-in said he wore a beard. Even if the guy had stubble rather than a full beard, as the wife claimed, Jake's beard could be a stick-on disguise.

She kept her mouth zipped.

'Do you live nearby?'

'Yeah, about a K, too.' True, except that she pointed towards Luisa's house in the west. 'That way.'

They sealed the mugs to finish their coffee post-workout, before Nessa pushed Jake through her toughest routine, satisfied when he fell to the ground starfish-style and whimpered, 'I surrender.'

She offered him a hand up, laughing.

After they'd stretched and drained their drinks, he took her mug. 'I missed you over the last few days.'

Nessa's face warmed stupidly again. She normally had strong instincts about people that were spot on, but Jake was messing with her head.

'Be here tomorrow?'

She kept it vague. 'Hope so.'

'You know what I love most about training at this time of day? You see some interesting things on the way here.'

Nessa smiled. He probably thought she agreed, but she always jogged from home to the park with blinkers on, focused on the workout ahead.

'Drunks staggering home, domestics, people going out to work, crooks coming home from work–'

She froze, except for her racing heartbeat. Had Jake just thrown out a *catch me if you can*?

Or was he as nice as he seemed and really had seen crooks in action? Had he spotted her home intruder?

'God, where did you say you live?' Her chuckle sounded odd in her ears. 'My area doesn't have crims.'

She hoped he swallowed the act.

'Top end of Barley Street. And you'd be surprised. I see dodgy stuff *all the time.*'

Her head cocked. She had to force it level. Surely he was challenging her?

Jake suddenly checked his watch, then made a suction noise with his tongue and teeth. 'We have a big job on in the city today and I've gotta get on-site.'

He looked shattered, which she didn't swallow. He'd obviously sensed her suspicion and gone into fast-backpedal-mode. Too late, buster.

She observed him take off in the direction of Barley Street North, suspecting that Jake would be busy two mornings from now. Either he wouldn't show for their workout or he'd have done his business beforehand.

Come to think of it, hadn't he worn an extra twinkle in his eye the morning of Luisa's robbery? That was the day he'd pushed for her name and jumped into her workout. Was that because he was on a high after the break-in? Maybe even because he knew she was a cop and he had one over her?

Nessa's eyes burned into Jake's back as he fled. She was determined to nab him before he hurt someone. The next homeowner that interrupted him might be less robust than Luisa or Smythe and have a heart attack.

She laid plans every spare minute until midnight on Thursday finally arrived.

Donned in black tracksuit, black beanie, black gloves and even an old pair of black sneakers, she was still worried that a neighbour might spot her and call the cops. It'd be just her luck if Big Phil took the job.

If anything, that thought bolstered Nessa while she jogged to the top end of Barley Street. She squeezed into a bushy shrub, gagging on the stench of the crushed flowers. It reminded her of one of her first tasks in the job: clearing used condoms after an illicit sex-drugs-and-dance party, fortunately armed with long tongs and Vicks rubbed under her nostrils. She repressed a sneeze, wishing she had some of the menthol ointment now, and scoped the scene.

Based on the crook's recent jobs, he chose detached homes with a side gate through which he entered, exited, or both. That eliminated two sets of units and a handful of townhouses, along with the place she'd chosen as her base. This spot gave her the greatest camouflage and best view of the houses she considered most vulnerable.

If her theory was right.

A shiver of doubt started deep in her gut, chased by a rush of adrenaline through her body, a corresponding surge in her heartbeat and dryness in her mouth. The same symptoms she'd felt before competing in her first fun run. Fear being overcome by excitement and expectation.

The job *would* go down tonight.

What if she'd misjudged the location, though?

Her eyes narrowed. Her crook was either dumb, and therefore predictable, or playing *catch me if you can* and conceited enough to want a close shave, which made him dumb enough to underestimate Nessa.

Either way, it'd happen around here. If she didn't spot the entry, she hoped the homeowner would discover the crook in the act. In the quietness of night in this sleepy suburb, she'd hear a scream or shout and probably manage to head off the crook. Their guy travelled on foot and Nessa was a fast runner with excellent endurance these days.

All good, providing the vic didn't have that heart attack.

She nestled into the shrub to take some weight off her feet. This could take a while.

An hour later, she dodged a ciggie butt thrown into her hideout by a dog walker.

Half an hour after that, Nessa's feet hurt from being stationary so long.

By 2.30am, she resorted to tugging on the ties of her windcheater for amusement.

Twenty minutes on, she needed to pee. She knew boredom and bladders had stuffed up many surveillance ops. Surviving both tonight would be good preparation for detective training.

She managed to hold on, cross-eyed, for forty more minutes before squatting in desperation, mouth-breathing to avoid inhaling ammonia mixed with the stench of the bush.

At 3.45am, her heart thudded. It had to happen soon.

Nessa sneezed and for that split second her eyes shut. When she opened them, she saw Jake jog from one of the houses, just as she heard a female yell, loud and shrill, followed by the bang of a gate.

Another person sprinted in the same direction as Jake, passing him a moment later. Nessa noted they were of similar build and this one wore a backpack.

She bolted after them, yelling, 'Stop! Police!'

The two men threw her a glance, then ran on. Jake scooped an object off the ground. The other kept going but slower and with a limp.

Nessa repeated her warning.

She came abreast of Jake, the buzz of the chase clouded by the hurt on his face. As they ran together, she said, 'Jake, I'm sorry. I'm not in childcare.'

'I just clicked. Are you after Cinderella?'

Matching her pace, he tossed her a sneaker.

She grasped it smoothly, then checked out the guy ahead, whose gait combined a stagger-roll-jog. He'd be easy to catch. 'As a matter of fact, I am.'

'Before you go...'

She half-turned. 'Yeah?'

'I'm fine with you being a cop. So, can I take you to dinner sometime?'

Heat prickled her cheeks, as she nodded. 'We'll talk at the park tomorrow.'

Nessa watched Jake spring up, clicking his heels together.

She jogged on to stoop over her crook, who'd collapsed on the bitumen. She badged him, grinning. 'You're busted, Cinderella!'

THE JOB II

Some things can't be unseen...or unfelt, unsmelt, or unheard
They churn in your gut
bang in your brain like wet towels in a dryer
drip off your tongue too quickly or stick in your throat, impossible
to say
Can't sleep because the flashbacks are worse
imprinted on the inside of your eyelids they play over and over and
over again
too loud, too bright, too clear, too horrific
Might be the end of the line, think this might be the point of no
return
But trading the blue uniform for jeans and a flanny shirt
filling in the days reading, listening to the radio, watching the footy,
pottering in the garden
while crackles on the radio, wet knees from crouching on the
ground, a familiar face, a child's bike, a foggy day or just breathing
could trigger a flashback
Sometime, anytime, it will all come back
too loud, too bright, too clear, too horrific

IMPACT

Finalist in the international
2012 *Cutthroat* Rick DeMarinis Short Story Contest

IMPACT

Tony McCain cornered without slowing. His offsider gripped the dash and braced while she spoke into the mike over the clamour of the siren, updating their ETA.

The sergeant's spine cracked as they took the hairpin bend.

Down the long straight, around one more corner.

Central communications had relayed a sketchy report. A vehicular collision with a pushbike. The location. Minimum of one serious injury. The anonymous male witness refused to remain on the scene or elaborate. Every instinct from twenty-nine years in the job told McCain it'd be gruesome.

He glimpsed the young constable in the passenger seat. Her face was dappled in the premature dusk of winter and he saw that a curly tuft of black hair escaped her bun. A strange thing to notice, in the circumstances.

His mind made another odd sidestep. Sara Pratt. If ever there was someone who didn't fit their surname, she sat next to him in the divvy van. Alert, sensible, resourceful, certainly not foolish, he could see her advancing her career in any direction and quickly. Maybe she'd be the next female chief commissioner. He hoped she wouldn't end up crucified if she made it to the top.

Politics and policing, oil and water, greasy like the wet bitumen under the van's tyres, and it was why he stayed in the operational side of coppering. He could have gone for promotions, but he joined the force to help the community, not sit behind a poncy desk, shuffling files.

His mouth twitched as he acknowledged his habit of deflecting from the situation ahead. He inhaled through his nostrils and figured they'd confront it soon enough. In less than two minutes in fact.

Hold it together, man.

He was trying to. But he knew a string of young families near the address. Too tragic to think the pushbike belonged to a kid he trained at basketball or one of his groupies at the local pre-school or primary school he visited with the station's 'little red car'. Once a month he talked to 'his kids' about all things policing, from cyber-bullying to safe cycling.

Safe cycling.

A mental image struck of his front-row favourites at the pre-school: Lily, Bella, and Zac.

Too young to be out on the road. His shoulders loosened. Then he took a sharp breath. *Unless it was a driveway incident.*

A sharp pain stabbed his eye. McCain white-knuckled the steering wheel and focused on driving.

Seconds later, his brain resumed its jumping jacks. He'd often smugly thought that working hands-on in the hills outstripped his previous flat-land postings. Here his team tackled country policing in suburbia. They managed a population of 700-odd households with a transient tourist count of over a million each year, which made every shift varied and community oriented.

Today reminded him of the flipside of living and working in an intimate neighbourhood. He wasn't a born-again nutter, but he prayed: *God, let the vics be tourists, not locals.*

The road dipped. The fog thickened and wrapped around the blue-and-white, limiting visibility to mere metres.

'Are you ready, Sara?'

Despite the siren, radio, and road noise, he sounded too loud. And he could smell his offsider's perfume. His senses were in overdrive.

'Yes, Sarge.'

Two controlled words. Apprehensive, yet professional, Pratt was as ready as she could be.

McCain unconsciously twisted his gold wedding band as their fog lamps flared on a yellow warning sign at the final curve. He made the turn, easing off the accelerator.

His guts plummeted.

Fog lamps illuminated the scene as he braked.

He stopped, diagonally blocking the thoroughfare.

Nissan Patrol and pushbike.

He groaned, raking fingers through thin, more-salt-than-pepper hair.

'Jesus,' Sara whispered.

Compressed like a piano accordion, a pink pushbike lay metres from the SUV. Incongruously, its holographic handlebar streamers fluttered in the icy wind and one purple training wheel spun slowly.

The Nissan driver blocked the rest of their view. He'd crumpled to the wet bitumen, head in hands. Something infiltrated his shock. It could've been the flashing red-and-blue lights on their vehicle or the screech of McCain's door.

Before alighting, Sara alerted D24 to their arrival.

McCain heard her ask, 'ETA on the ambos?' and moved beyond earshot.

The driver rose, stumbled but righted himself. Ashen faced, his hands shook visibly from ten metres away.

'I didn't...I couldn't...I *couldn't* stop!'

As the man shifted, McCain saw shiny black shoes with

primrose bows, topped by pink ankle socks with sky-blue bobbles.

'She came out of nowhere! Like a bat out of hell.'

McCain took in stick-thin legs. His mind in hyper-state, he grasped the pose was too slack and still. A cop's nightmare is an incident where little kiddies are injured. Almost thirty years in the job and yet, as he mentally processed the scene, his stomach flipped.

Sara hurried to the driver. She laid a hand on his shoulder and spoke in a gentle tone. The man bent forwards, sobbing into his chest.

The sarge ignored them and moved to the little girl.

Only about thirty seconds had elapsed since their arrival, but time slowed, and detail amplified.

He gazed again at the socks, then her multi-hued pleated skirt, woolly pink vest, and raspberry T-shirt with frilly sleeves.

Not for the first time at an accident, McCain wished he could rewind the clock and somehow prevent it.

His eyes flicked to the child's delicate hands. They lay supine. Her soft white palms speckled with red droplets and road grit.

McCain drew a deep breath a metre from the body. So close, he could smell and almost taste blood.

The little girl's eyes were open.

And vacant.

Fingers gripped his bicep, forcing him around.

The driver pummelled him. McCain took it for a few moments, until Sara reached for the man and led him away.

'She came from nowhere.' The man's voice broke. 'Looking over her shoulder, not at the road. There was nothing I could do. You have to believe me! It happened too fast.'

McCain knelt. His knees cracked. He placed two fingers on the girl's neck, feeling for a pulse. None, but he hadn't thought there would be. He leaned close to check her airway. As he tilted her head back, the mass of contusions across her pixie face shut down his brain.

Then it became clear. He knew this child.

Oh, God. No.

They were all trained to perform CPR with the option to do just compressions. But as if he had a choice when it came to a kiddie.

He ran through it in his mind. *Thirty compressions. Two effective breaths. No stopping.*

'How long for the ambos?' he called to Sara, before placing his hands on the little girl's chest and commencing compressions.

'Nine minutes.' She touched his arm. 'I think she's gone, boss.'

He shrugged her off. 'I'm not playing God. We do everything we can until the ambos take over. Got it?'

She hunkered beside him. 'I'll breathe.'

They worked robotically, counting, breathing, pumping.

McCain focused on his hand position and compression rhythm.

He dimly heard Sara's voice, '…twenty-seven, twenty-eight, twenty-nine, thirty…' and counted two beats while she exhaled, making the slender chest rise under his hands. Each time, he sent up a prayer for a spontaneous sign of life. Each time, his heart constricted further.

The firies beat the ambos. A patrol car joined the line-up with two of their blokes. Onlookers gathered, shocked, yet transfixed, unable to turn away from a sight that would haunt their dreams. While the cops tried to breathe life back into the limp body, the rest of the emergency crew settled into the industry of disaster.

Control the crowd.

Secure the area.

Set up detours.

Pratt and McCain kept breathing and pumping until the paramedics arrived and took over. Hope sparked with a brief return of beat on the monitor but even as the ambos loaded the child into their truck, the veteran cop knew she'd be DOA.

The ambulance disappeared, lights and bells screaming.

Only then did McCain say to his constable, 'It's *Bella*.'

Their breaths plumed in the frosty air. The light seeping from the glazed fanlight above the front door gave it an ethereal look, jarring with the reason for their call. Sara's pulse pounded in her temples as they waited.

'Are you sure you want to do this, Sarge? You don't have to. I can handle it. Or Patto can come with me if you like.'

'It's my responsibility.' McCain's voice was cut glass, his face puffy, although the redness had subsided.

Sara had witnessed the boss fight emotion and frustration on occasion. He'd once whacked a brick wall so hard he fractured his pinkie. But until today, she'd never seen him bawl and wished the memory could be erased.

When the ambulance tore away, and he named the local child, she saw him lose it. The signs: stricken eyes, taut jaw line, and quivering mouth. She'd dragged him to the van and let him cry, realising he'd hate their colleagues or the firies to see his breakdown. She had patted his arm, muttered the usual well-meant but essentially futile placations, and predicted they wouldn't talk of it. Ever.

Now, she simply nodded and adjusted her hat.

Her palms moistened when a bright light came on overhead, the handle cranked, and the door swung. She wiped them on her pants. Notifications were never easy but having to tell parents about their pre-schooler's death had to be the worst.

'Mr Avery?'

'Yes.' The tall, polo-necked man squinted at Sara, then past her. 'Tony?'

Sara wondered at his calmness. Sure, he seemed curious, perplexed even, as to why they were on his doorstep. Yet, he acted far from alarmed.

Oh, hell. She gulped bile. They'd failed to raise the parents on the landline and anticipated it was because they were searching for their daughter.

They have no idea she was even missing. No clue what's coming.

She said, 'Can we come in?'

Michael Avery smoothed his eyebrow with manicured fingers, then gestured to inside. 'Yes, of course.'

They trailed him into a formal lounge.

'Come in. Sit.'

They perched on a white sofa that was too low and hard.

The sarge managed, 'Is Julia home?'

As the husband said, 'She's just...' Sara glanced through to the kitchen and noticed an array of green shopping bags. A woman with bobbed strawberry-blonde hair moved into view and did a double-take.

With bottles of tomato sauce and olive oil in each hand, she rushed into the living room.

'Tony?' She addressed McCain. 'Is everything okay?'

When the boss's mouth flapped mutely, Sara said, 'Mrs Avery, Mr Avery. I'm Sara Pratt and you know Tony McCain.'

Polite murmurs and nods followed by rote.

She started the terrible part. 'It's Bella.'

The woman's shoulders relaxed. 'Bella? She's upstairs, having a little nap, isn't she, Mike?'

'Mrs Avery,' Sara cut in. 'Bella's not upstairs.'

'What?' The sauce dropped onto the pristine white carpet as the mother covered her mouth.

'Julia!'

The husband's sharp reproach seemed excessive. The

bottle had splintered on impact, its contents splattering the shag pile – but what was tomato sauce on the carpet compared with their daughter's well-being?

Julia froze, except for her eyes, which darted between her husband and the nestled bottle. Her soft-rose complexion drained to waxen.

Maybe they're reacting to us, not the sauce. We're oozing an aura of doom.

Still mulling whether the sauce, their presence, or the three words *Bella's not upstairs* had rattled the couple more, Sara guided the woman to the sofa. Crouched before the parents, she scanned to McCain but the sarge remained impotent.

'Mr and Mrs Avery, we have very bad news concerning Bella.'

Michael rose and yelled, 'Bella, come here!'

His wife's knees trembled. Her pressed pants made a rustling sound.

'Mike, sit down.' At last, McCain had found his voice. 'Bella's not upstairs.'

'Not possible. You,' Julia frowned at her husband, 'you said Bella was tired and needed a nap. That's why I couldn't get through to you about the chops; you had the phone on silent so she could rest.'

She dashed upstairs. They heard her footsteps above them. Doors opened and closed, and her cries grew more frantic.

Sara shadowed her to the base of the staircase. As she hovered, uncertain, her boss said, 'Best give her a moment.'

She nodded and sat again, listening to Julia's agitated motion, and watching the husband. There was something a little odd about him. Then again, there's no textbook reaction to sudden loss. The one certainty in a death knock: they must be prepared for anything and everything, including denial, anguish, and aggression.

'Where is she, Mike?' The woman's pupils glinted hard and black against pasty skin as she lurched down the last treads.

The knees of her pants were creased now as if she'd been crawling on the floor, searching under beds for her daughter.

Her husband lifted his palms helplessly. He approached her, reached out. She flinched but allowed him to lead her to the sofa.

Sara gave McCain's foot a discreet nudge. He got it. They stood together.

'Little Bella isn't here. We have very bad news about her.'

The words sounded awkward and inadequate in Sara's ears. She'd practised phantom scenarios in bed since her academy days and been part of two reality dramas on jobs, although never as the informant, yet the script felt wrong.

She dug her nails into her palms, to sharpen her wits. 'I'm...we're very sorry, but your daughter has been involved in a fatal collision this afternoon–'

'But how–?'

'It appears that she rode her bicycle into the path of an oncoming four-wheel drive.'

She omitted that the kid cycled onto the road 'like a bat out of hell' according to the driver, shooting backward glances, oblivious to all else. She'd find a kinder way to explain after their initial shock.

'Unfortunately–' Sara's body iced, and her tongue thickened, slurring the word. She tried again. 'Unfortunately, the driver couldn't avoid impact with Bella. We attended the scene and an ambulance arrived quickly after.'

The parents drilled her eyes with theirs.

'Every effort was made to revive your daughter, but... I'm...we're so sorry to tell you, she died.'

Julia mouthed *my baby* and her husband tried to embrace her.

Sara paused for the parents to absorb what she'd told

them, giving opportunity for the sarge to belatedly take the lead. She reflected upon tragedy and the way it solidified some families, shattered others. When Julia cringed from her husband, she figured them for the latter.

And so, the waves of the impact would continue to crash. Foremost affected were Bella's loved ones, of course. But the poor driver and his family would be irrevocably altered, too. Along with each person who saw or touched the broken child – the other emergency service workers, tow-truck driver, civilian onlookers, right down to the mortician who prepared her for burial.

Sara flashed to the sarge's grey face. He looked suddenly old. Her stomach knotted. *Please don't let this push him into early retirement.*

At length, she and McCain let themselves out of the Avery residence. Sara's gaze fixed on the toes of her boots as they trod to the van. Inside the cabin, she looked through the rain-speckled window. A curtain twitched on the picture window of the formal lounge. She couldn't see if the mother or father stood there.

McCain fired the engine and slowly reversed. As the house receded, sadness pulled at Sara's chest. She recalled the mother shrinking further over the duration of the interview and visualised her recoil when they gave more detail of the incident and mentioned formal identification of the body and an inquest. The solitary instance Julia became animated was when she asked what Bella was wearing – which the boss described in disturbing detail. That last-ditch hope crushed, she'd dropped into an uncommunicative state, while her husband sobbed tearlessly.

Julia let the curtain swish into place. The vile white drapes, in the white-walled mausoleum of a living room, with its rigid white couch, white sateen throw cushions and stupid white shaggy carpet. All a pose, all of which she'd agreed to in order to keep the peace. As she always did. She'd spent half of Bella's life chasing the child out of this room to keep it pristine and please her husband.

The surge of anger fizzled.

What she would give to see Bella streak through, brush her finger-paint plastered hands over everything.

She turned away from the window, her actions unsteady. From the corner of her eye she glimpsed Bella peep from behind the island bar.

A burst of joy died in the next beat.

She would never again see her baby play peek-a-boo. Smell her sweet, freshly shampooed hair. Hear her giggle. Or feel her slender arms drape around her neck.

Her heart tore anew.

Michael hadn't moved from the sofa. She had too much pain inside to worry about him. Instead, she gathered the mugs and stacked them in the dishwasher.

Better. Better to be busy. Better not to think.

She hummed. Low. Tuneless. With occasional catches in her throat.

'Julia.'

He touched her. Her nerve endings were raw, and she shrieked, pulling away.

The kitchen floor needs a mop. I'll scrub the grout. Hot, hot water.

'Julia… Listen…'

She looked through her husband and scuttled into the laundry.

In her fog, she failed to notice the bucket fill and overflow or even the bloom of angry red as boiling water seared her hand.

The man couldn't shut off what had happened. He didn't think he'd ever get behind a steering wheel again. His hand shook so hard that liquid sloshed over the rim. His gaze followed the drips of beer onto the carpet, equally incapable of dealing with it as he was unable to drink from or put down the glass.

It was plucked from his fingers.

'Come on, love,' his wife whispered. 'It's after midnight. Let's go to bed.'

He tried to reply but made only a garbled noise.

She hugged him. Rubbed his back and murmured. He cried. His body shuddered.

'I just can't believe it,' he managed to say.

His wife leaned back and stroked away the tears on his cheeks. Fresh ones streaked.

'I know, I know.'

'My bloody truck killed her. It's my fault.'

'No, it's not.'

She held down his hands. He hadn't realised he was throwing his arms around.

'It *is*. If I hadn't been driving...'

She pressed a finger to his lips. 'The little girl rode out in front of you. She wasn't paying attention. There was no way you could stop. You said it yourself, love. And the police understand what happened. Nobody's blaming you.'

'*I am.*'

He squeezed his eyes shut, watched the impact again in slow motion and moaned.

She shushed him, embracing him harder than before.

His next moan erupted and echoed in the quiet house.

'Try not to wake the kids.'

She had spoken gently, but he fired back, 'At least our kids *can* wake up.'

He jumped to his feet, grasped the beer, downed the liquid in one and hurled the glass against the wall.

It shattered and sprayed glittering fragments.

The night crept slowly to morning. She couldn't contemplate sleep, although Michael went to bed directly after they returned from the morgue. She didn't get it. Even though it was long after midnight, how could he sleep after seeing their dead baby?

For a long while, Julia stood in the centre of Bella's room, rotating slowly, then frantically. The rainbow of colours and images blended as in a kaleidoscope.

She collapsed onto the play rug and dug her fingers into its pink pile. Pink was Bella's favourite colour.

Several times she held her breath, desperate to float away to be with Bella, but her body denied her. Involuntarily, she gasped and breathed.

Still no tears came. She wondered how someone could feel numb yet hurt everywhere. How her eyes could burn as acutely as the blistered scald on her hand but stay dry, empty.

Through those bloodshot eyes, she stared at Bella's wall. A butterfly-patterned umbrella hung on a peg by its curved hook, alongside an anorak, long scarf, and cape.

All of her baby's most treasured winter items.

Next, she gazed at the hot pink gumboots, upside down on their rack, and a pair of fluffy slippers. The gap between them belonged to a pair of dress shoes, the shoes Bella wore today – *no, yesterday.*

Exhausted but sleepless, Julia lay on Bella's single bed. She buried her face into the doona, pillow, pyjamas. She drank in the sweet scent of her child, then her fingernails wrenched at the skin over her heart.

Later, her cheek rested on the mattress. She clung to the pillow, her eyes fixed forwards.

Bella loved to paint and draw. Her pictures were typical

four-year-old stuff: unsophisticated stick figures, vividly coloured. A little girl holding her mum's hand, both donned in pink triangle dresses. A big white house outlined in black crayon, trees, grass and flowers, mum and child playing catch. At the seaside, massive beaming sun, tricoloured umbrella, two beach towels, mum and daughter building a sandcastle.

It was the first time she'd noted a recurring theme.

Sara pulled on the handbrake. She sat for a moment, thinking, observing. Many descriptors jumped to mind: contemporary, stark white, extensive glass, expensive, cold. A house, not a home – it was far too large and imposing for a family of three.

She corrected 'a family of three' to 'a childless couple', shivered and left the cocoon of the divvy van.

At the front door, she flashed back to waiting here yesterday. She felt much older this afternoon. The experience of looking after the boss and managing the death knock had matured her more than any previous twenty-four hours of policing.

Sara pressed the doorbell and after a minute, knocked on the frame.

No response.

She tracked around the house, checked windows, and came to French doors at the rear. She peered through and spied Julia seated at the island bar in the kitchen. The mother was pallid and dressed the same as yesterday. She clutched a small stuffed toy and stared into the distance.

Sara tapped and waited. Then she called gently, 'Mrs Avery? Julia?' and let herself in.

Julia stirred and turned. Her forehead creased when Sara placed her hat on the bench before her eyes glazed.

Sara fixed the woman a coffee and the movement or aroma eventually roused Julia.

'Oh, you. Sara?'

'Yes, that's right. Sara Pratt. I was on patrol nearby and wanted to see how you're doing.'

The mother shrugged, signifying no words could describe how she was doing. Sara had messed that up.

'Is Michael home?'

Julia shook her head.

'Is someone here with you?'

After a pause, Julia said, 'I sent Mum home. Same for the others who came with their *casseroles* and well-meaning *bullshit*.'

She had sparked up with that sentence, but Sara saw her vanish again. She tried to draw the woman into conversation. It was a constant battle against suffocating grief.

Nonetheless, the constable persevered. She had questions. The sarge didn't know she was here. Maybe he'd back her all the way or maybe he'd haul her over the coals. It didn't matter because he'd trained her to investigate anything that made her nose twitch.

And it twitched like a bunny's now because the story didn't add up.

So, Sara prodded cautiously. It was poor timing for the mum but critical to the investigation, even if everyone else was calling it 'the accident'.

'Was yesterday the first time Bella went off on her bike alone?'

Julia passed a hand over her eyes as if blocking the image. She shook her head, yet replied, 'I think so.'

Sara talked of other things awhile, then circled back. 'She was a tiny thing. Didn't feel the cold?'

Dressed as she was, on a freezing winter's day, Bella must have been of hearty mountain stock.

The mother angled her head. 'We keep the house this hot for Bella.'

She lifted and dropped a hand.

Sara saw her slip away again and asked a final question.

'So, when will Michael be home? I'd like to have a chat with him, too…'

Red-veined eyes swivelled to hers.

They held a long look.

'I don't know.'

At nightfall, she trudged up the stairs and down again.

She placed the items on the floor in front of him. He lowered his gaze to the pathetic pile.

'You want to tell me why my daughter–' Julia's voice caught. She swallowed and said, 'Why my daughter was outside, at dusk, in winter, wearing a skirt and T-shirt? Two degrees and she goes for a ride in her best shoes and socks, without her coat?' She picked up her baby's anorak and stretched again to retrieve the set of pink gumboots. 'And without her boots?'

'*What?*' Michael's eyes widened.

Julia's thoughts strayed to dried mud from the tiny gumboots that marred the pretentious shagpile. Her eyelids fluttered and her lips curved briefly.

Mouth flatlined again, she pressed, 'And why you thought my daughter was upstairs having a nap, when she was actually riding her bike, by herself?'

'I *thought* she was upstairs.'

Her breath hissed through her teeth. She drew his eyes into her soul.

'Come.'

Something—her hard expression or her lack of fear—

inverted their usual roles and he followed. They walked through the internal door to the garage.

She tossed him the car keys. 'Drive.'

The roller door lifted. Michael reversed. The door slid closed while she watched numbly.

At the top of the steep driveway, she instructed, 'Our lookout.'

Her husband nodded and pulled left. She jabbed off the radio, halting a love song.

They reached Five-Ways and parked with the engine running, the heater ineffectual against the frigidness inside her.

The car park was otherwise empty—the tourists either tucked up in restaurants, B&Bs or gone—and completely dark. There were no streetlights here and the fog was a pea-souper. Their headlamps barely illuminated past the safety barrier, but Julia pictured the carpet of lawn, the canopy of trees far down the hill and the catchment dam further beyond.

'I should have known. But it took this,' she waved, 'for me to realise.' The words quivered.

After a long pause, she went on, 'Bella wasn't just a mummy's girl, clingy, going through a stage. That wasn't why she always wanted to be with me, why she didn't want to stay with you when I went shopping yesterday.'

Another piece of her heart broke. She forced herself to breathe. It didn't matter what happened to her later – she needed to finish this.

'True, Michael?'

She shuddered over his name.

'Things changed after we had the baby. You were obsessive-compulsive with me and Bella, but I thought you didn't have the greatest role models, so it wasn't your fault. I put it down to you just not *getting* parenting. I never realised what you *really* were.'

Julia chafed her arms. 'Maybe that makes me as bad as you.' Her tone coarsened. 'No, I'm *not*.'

He shifted to look at her. She fixed on a leaf stuck to the windscreen.

'Are you going to tell me what happened yesterday?'

'You know what–'

She cut him off. 'Here's what I think. I think Bella was running away.' She glanced at him. 'From you.'

She turned back to the leaf above the wiper. 'Well?'

She hammered him until he stuttered, 'Oh, but, it's…I thought she'd hidden in the garden. Really, I did.'

Her poor baby wasn't safe in her own home.

'Huh. Maybe I believe you. But I think—no, I *know*—that you bullied us because you're too much of a goddamn pussy to stand up to your Type A parents.'

She changed tack. 'That policewoman came back today. Sara Pratt.' She studied him. 'She's smart, that one. She's suss about the details. She asked about *you*.'

He cringed, confirmation she expected but didn't want. She faced forward.

'I wasn't certain until she came around. I'd started to piece it together, though. From Bella's anorak and gumboots, initially. Then I noticed something in her bedroom. *Not one* of her pictures has a man in it. There is no *dad*. Only a mum and daughter. Me and Bella. Or us and her nana. Nothing of *you*.'

'But–'

'Shut up. You don't get to talk. *Yet.* Anyway, so things were dropping into place and I remembered how strangely Bella always acted after she'd been alone with you. And Pratt sealed it.'

She realised she'd been grinding her teeth and unclenched her jaw.

Michael sat stiffly.

'Pratt would break you in five minutes. And even if you

did bluff your way past her, there's no way that you'd survive a coroner's inquest.'

She glared at the leaf.

'And there's no way I'm going to let it be known what sort of *man*,' she grimaced, 'you are.'

'What are you on about? Stupid woman.' He'd reverted to type: intimidating. Then he faked outrage with, 'Just what the hell are you insinuating? I didn't do anything bad.'

She answered with a repulsed snort.

He switched to pleading. 'I promise you. I just played around...'

In her peripheral vision, lit by the luminous green of the dash lights, she saw his hands flutter.

Julia's stomach pitched. She pushed down the vomit. She wouldn't leave a trace of being in the car tonight.

As one part of her mind raged, another hoped he was telling the truth – that the post-mortem wouldn't find evidence of sexual assault. They wouldn't prove anything, concluding that Bella's imaginary race and limited road sense led to an awful accident.

Her hand pulled the lever. The door released but instead of alighting, she said, 'You're too weak to go to jail.'

She twisted sideways, pointed a finger at his temple and said, 'So, you're going to gun the engine of this fancy-dancy midlife-crisis sports car of yours and you're going to point its nose down the reservoir road. No steering, no braking. Accelerate full power.'

He nodded and sobbed.

'Because you're too much of a coward to go to jail and let some arsehole do to you what you did to my daughter.'

'I only–'

'Even if you only...' she faltered, nauseated, unable to repeat his words. 'We both know what you *would've* done to her if she'd lived, sooner or later.'

She stumbled out and before she slammed the door

snarled, 'Don't worry, you won't make it past the Elbow alive.'

Devil's Elbow, the local nickname for the sharp corner on the steep hill. And hideously appropriate.

Julia walked in the direction of their empty home. She heard the BMW crawl forward, then give a sharp rev before it launched down the plunging gravel roadway.

It seemed a long interval before she heard the impact. One mountain ash would do the job and the thicket of trees at the Elbow guaranteed success.

Tears curled from the sides of both eyes. The fog enveloped her.

Now she could grieve for Bella.

The stone church was packed for the funeral, with every seat filled. Not even standing room remained. Pressed against the cold back wall, McCain stood shoulder-to-shoulder with his wife Sally, and Sara Pratt, three figures in their immaculate police uniforms among a sea of others garbed in blue: every available member from their station, plus their counterparts from the neighbouring towns and even a few from further afield.

Sara's back and shoulders were set, her body so tight she barely seemed to breathe. In contrast, Sally's chest and belly lifted and deflated with her inhales and exhales in McCain's side vision. *Inhale, exhale, repeat.* She swore the technique was the reason she'd survived the worst of the job; the only way she could present a façade of calm while screaming and swearing mutely.

McCain blinked eyes dry from too much whisky, too many tears, and too little sleep. His gaze fell on the infants perched on the steps below the altar, their expressions ranging from bewildered to miserable.

He looked away and screwed his eyes shut, but instead of blanking the kids' pain, he pictured Bella, her broken body, and her broken bike.

Hold it together, man.

He opened his eyelids, determined to be strong for his colleagues, his shattered community and Bella's loved ones. At least for today. He couldn't think beyond that, though. Wasn't sure he could ever return from stress leave.

Not wanting to, and yet unable to stop himself, McCain's eyes travelled to Julia standing at the front of the church. Her shoulder blades were sharp bumps inside her heavy woollen coat as her body bowed forward, her hands resting on the end of the shiny, undersized white casket, her fingertips pointing to the large portrait of her daughter.

Alone, when by rights she should have had her husband for support. But him dead, too.

God help me.

McCain wished Sara had never shared her theory with him and he was relieved they couldn't prove it. Not a witness or piece of physical evidence so far pointing to anything but Bella's death being a terrible accident and Michael's a suicide – his inability to cope with the tragic loss of his child.

But Sara was born for the job; she had good instincts. And deny it all he liked, but McCain's gut agreed. Michael's single-car fatal accident and today's funeral for only Bella were no coincidence.

Beside him, Sara took an audible breath, clearly steeling herself, as the minister comforted Julia. She had admitted regrets: ignoring her impulse to check on the parents and delaying her return for further questions until the very time Michael wrapped his BMW around a tree.

God help him, McCain was glad she'd been too late. Maybe the one good impact of Bella's accident was her father's death.

THE JOB III

It's common knowledge, isn't it?
Most crooks are dumb
They make mistakes—lots of them—because no education from CSI-this-that-or-the-other, or their last cellmate, is going to make up for what they just aren't capable of grasping
It's only the 'easy life' until they get caught
And they will get caught because they're not the sharpest tools in the shed
That's why they're crooks
Get the picture?
Mind you, they keep me in a job – a job I mostly love, though I miss the action now that I'm typically chained to the desk
So, sometimes I take a patrol
It's like the good old days again
Riding the van, educating a rookie, slowing down the lead foots, all the while on alert for a call, or anything suss, reason to give the strobes and siren a whirl
C'mon, crooks, do your best
But expect to be caught, so work on your story
Surprise us: anything but 'I'm your boss' or 'I wasn't doing anything wrong'

Make it good
Make it a cracker
Make our day
Get the picture?

HOT PATROL

First published as 'Hot Job' in *The Foothills Magazine* December 2013–February 2014 edition

HOT PATROL

Sally swiped her nape and grimaced at her slick fingers. It was nowhere near the hottest part of summer, either.

Not that it was scorching. More, uncomfortable. Sticky inside the uniform, her undies were sweaty, and her hair had frizzed into red pipe-cleaners. The night was airless but not oppressive enough that they would be inundated with alcohol-fuelled domestics or need to patrol for match-happy larrikins. But there was a full moon and that invariably drew the local NUPHYs out of the woodwork.

Her eyebrows lifted at her non-PC slip. *Tut-tut. Most improper to label a punter with 'needs urgent psychological help yesterday'…even if the straightjacket fits.*

Sally snorted and almost wished they would be besieged with such callouts. Anything would be an improvement on the old clock-watch and paperwork-push in the station.

The desk sergeant waved as he passed her open door. He hitched and rolled his stiff leg, the legacy of an encounter with a sledgehammer-wielding customer thirteen years ago that had ended his active duty.

Sally screwed her face. She hadn't seen active duty in a long time. The thing about promotion, it's not until you have the new nameplate and extra stripes for senior sergeant that you realise you were much happier in operations than handling administrative–political bullshit.

There I go again with inappropriate thinking. She chuckled. *Shit, shoot me if I completely morph into a puppet to uptight policy.*

She clanged two gold coins into a mental piggy bank. The swear jar. Hubby Tony nicknamed her 'Trash Mouth' – a sure case of the pot calling the kettle black. Her Tony, who was also a cop, had a mouth on him, too. But thick skin and a trash mouth were prerequisites of their job. And he banked more than her every day.

A smile still in her eyes, she swigged from her water bottle, and observed the rookie attack a mountain of filing. He paused to smooth a hair, sighed, and plucked the next sheet.

The youngster, Paul Starr, appeared as brain-dead as she felt. That batch of filing equated to an apprentice cabinetmaker being sent to the hardware store for a left-handed screwdriver. But Starr needed to work that out for himself and wouldn't thank his boss, more particularly his female boss, for setting him straight.

Sally shut her yellow folder and lay her palm on top for a moment. She pressed down on the desk and heaved out of the chair.

Another thing Tony accused her of: comfortable married-woman spread. She blamed her ample girth on pen-pushing and assured him that his belly made a worthy rival. But he was right – she needed to get in shape. She'd be on par with fictional detective Henry Crabbe in *Pie in the Sky* if she took on a crook these days and would have to rely on outwitting, rather than outrunning.

Not a big ask, considering the IQ of the average crook.

Sally called, 'Mac, anything up?'

The desk sergeant gave a thumbs-down.

'P – Starr.'

Phew, close shave. Almost called him Porn Star, the moniker the crew gave their vain rookie after he'd hit on every female at the station save for her. He'd been with them about a month. Time she got to know him better.

'Ma'am?'

'Grab the van keys. We're hitting the road so I can get to know you while it's quiet.'

Mac and one of the other uniforms guffawed. Starr's olive complexion paled, and Sally beamed.

I do love parts of my job.

The first ten minutes went as well as a blind date. The rookie was on his best behaviour and duller than dishwater. But he soon settled down and even cracked a joke about a blonde trying to steal a police car. She laughed with him and decided the kid was growing on her.

Like a wart.

She sniggered and he looked bemused.

They coasted past St Joe's school and the oval. He turned onto the highway, then pulled into the car park at the Middle Hotel and did a slow drive through. Nothing was happening even there.

'Let's take a look-see at the Royal.'

As they proceeded towards the other pub nearby, their marked van stood out among the thin traffic, which slowed to fifty clicks. Sally smirked. All-so-innocent until they and the cop car diverged, then the lead foots would revert to their normal tricks.

Starr dropped the F-bomb, shot her an appalled glance and apologised. 'Sorry, ma'am. But it's bloody boring tonight, isn't it?'

'Yep,' she agreed. 'Not even a bloody jaywalker.'

Cha-ching in the swear jar.

They caught a red light at Dawson Street.

Starr drummed his fingers in time with their blinker and Sally murmured, 'So where's he off to?'

They viewed a tow truck with its ambers on flash bear in the Tecoma direction.

Their light changed and she blew out a breath. 'Follow it.'

The constable did a confused head tilt, then focused on merging back onto the highway.

Sally answered his unspoken question. 'Maybe he's en route to a breakdown. Or maybe he's on his way to the next call to come through our radio. Let's luck it.'

Starr grinned. 'The whole shebang?'

'Settle, Constable. Just shadow for now.'

He nodded, a nose twitch the single tell-tale of his disappointment at the vetoed strobes and siren.

The tow truck maintained a steady pace at five clicks under the varying speed limit as they traversed the foothills. Despite the continuous flash of amber, there was no sense of urgency.

The truck indicated right an instant before the next traffic light. The divvy van trailed. Still no matching incident report came through the radio or via the bat phone when Sally rang Mac.

She disconnected from Mac and commented, 'Where is this bloke going?'

The rookie shrugged.

They corkscrewed through steep and narrow streets. Two sets of headlights and the towie's flashers cut through the darkness. Even when they twisted onto a wider carriageway and the landscape rolled from residential to sweeping fields, they met few other vehicles in either direction. And the truck and van continued to drift.

Starr eyed his boss. She narrowed her gaze and signalled to persist.

A trickle of sweat dripped from her nose and she wiped it mechanically. Clock-watching and perspiration didn't rate against the scene in front of them. She sensed that action brewed.

The towie meandered once more into a built-up neighbourhood, then forked at the roundabout onto Dawson and completed a full circle.

Sally muttered, 'I think we got our NUPHY.'

Riveted on the road and truck ahead, Starr didn't react.

Sally radioed through. 'We seem to have ourselves a hot job. Driver acting suspiciously.'

She paused to double-check the seat next to the driver. Empty or occupied by someone bloody short. 'One head on board.' After updating their position, she called off.

'Move in. The whole shebang.'

'Pleasure, ma'am.'

The constable blinded her with his porno-worthy pearly whites.

In response to their red-and-blue lights and a *whoop* of the siren, the tow truck slowed. Then it accelerated. It swerved left at the Tourist Road and Sally groaned. Starr leaned forward.

The towie wasn't playing nice.

They couldn't cut him off on this section of the hill; it was too dangerous, notwithstanding the patchy traffic. If they tried to force him over and he misjudged the verge, the truck would skydive and eventually hurtle into a mountain ash.

Sally saw herself as fat man Crabbe.

Outwit, not outrun.

She visualised the surrounding terrain and the circuitous ride they'd just followed. Then she strategised, hoping he'd play straight into her hands. He turned right, taking the high road.

Dumb crook.

Sally pointed. 'We'll take the low road.'

'Why?'

'You'll see,' she told her rookie. 'I bet you a beer he's planning to lead us back to the highway.'

'But he's got at least three options once he reaches Hughes.'

'And I'm sure he'll return to where we've just been via the shortest route.'

Starr pursed his lips showing he was unconvinced. Luckily, he manoeuvred the van with a dexterity that impressed his superior more than his attitude.

They hovered at the Hughes Street intersection. And sure enough, a minute later the tow truck ambled into sight. Starr pulled the van across the road and the truck halted.

Sally said, 'You owe me a beer,' and hooked her finger at the constable. They approached the driver's door and she made a winding motion. The bloke dropped the window and peered down at them.

'Good evening.' The senior sergeant smiled as she took in the man's bare torso.

The driver replied, 'It is.' He seemed relaxed but for dilated pupils.

He glanced around Sally and pointed. 'Hey, pretty boy, love your fluoro vest.' He strummed his ribcage and added, 'It'd look good on me, don't ya reckon?'

The rookie flushed; his boss grinned on the inside.

'Where's the incident?' She pointed to the flashing amber bars.

The bloke cackled. 'I was hot and bored, what can I say?'

Definitely high. He hadn't blinked.

'Got your licence handy?'

'Woo-woo-woo-woo!' The sound vibrated as the man flapped a hand over his mouth.

Sally's neck jerked back in response.

What the bloody hell?

'Woo-woo-woo-woo!' With another battle cry, the bloke scrambled over the passenger seat and slithered through the window. The cops watched as he climbed onto the roof and beat it like a bongo drum in synch with the flashing lights.

'See what I see, Starr?'

He nodded mutely, floored by the driver's boxer shorts: black with three luminous pink arrows that pointed at a love heart over his crotch.

Classy.

'Our night just became a whole lot more entertaining,' she drawled. Then she shouted over the clamour, 'Make your way down, matey.'

The driver shrugged, yet instead of joining them, he re-entered the cabin via the far window.

'Licence please.'

'No can do.'

Sally frowned. 'It's at home?'

'Nope.'

'You don't have a licence?'

The bloke hooted his horn. A dog barked in reply, which set off a chorus of howls in the neighbourhood.

'That would be an affirmative.'

She hazarded, 'Unlicensed and this isn't your truck, right?'

He waved her nearer. 'You're so smart, you should be a cop.'

Another horn blast and a screech of laughter sent the dogs into a fresh yap-and-yelp contest.

'Oh, we have ourselves a *com-e-dian*.'

Sally straightened and hiked up her equipment belt around her marshmallow belly.

'Righto, how funny is it that you're taking a drug and alcohol test?'

She rolled her eyes as the man exited the truck and scaled the nearest gumtree.

'Think we could be in for a long time of it, Constable?' she asked her offsider.

'A long time and a good time,' Starr quipped with one of his gleaming grins.

THE JOB IV

*Hell, I hate these cases
they get right under the skin
Make me doubt I'm in the right job
although, what else would I do?
Make me doubt we make a difference
beyond clearance rates
or supporting victims' loved ones
It's not the stuff of superheroes
not likely to earn a medal, and honestly wouldn't want one
But finding the truth
putting away the culprit
is a good day in the office
Not much beats it
Hell…it's worth the pain*

LOSING HEIDI

Winner Scarlet Stiletto Awards 2014
Special Commendation

LOSING HEIDI

Hunger seemed irreverent in their business. But tell that to her empty gut.

Jude Reeve must've heard it rumble because she asked, 'When'd you last eat, boss?'

Inspector Rose Sturt squinted raw eyes at her colleague and shrugged. It was hours since she'd grabbed a pie, as her team caught this case back-to-back with wrapping up a nursing-home homicide.

'Suspected as much.' Reeve dropped a bag onto Sturt's desk.

'You're the best, Jude.'

With a mock-bow, Reeve handed her a small bottle. 'Because nobody delivers a salad roll and OJ like me?'

'Because you think of it.'

As they chewed, Sturt stretched her spine and hooked the desk lamp closer to a photograph of Jennifer Denton and her children. Now that her homicide inquiry was in hand, she could catch up on Reeve's background work on the Denton case.

'What've we got?'

'Not much.' Reeve gulped her orange juice and wiped her

lips with a serviette before she continued. 'Jennifer and Heidi were last seen outside the family home by Shelley Simpson, a mother in Heidi's playgroup, at the local supermarket on 13 May. Yet, according to Martin Denton, Jennifer's hubby, he last saw them at breakfast on Friday 14 May, the day Jennifer planned to visit her sister in Shepparton.'

'Did you check with the sister?' Sturt queried, as she flicked through the file.

'Uh-huh. Anna Gerald—the sister—says she didn't know anything about Jennifer and Heidi staying with her.'

The inspector pursed her lips.

Reeve seemed to read her mind. 'Anna was quite distraught when I spoke to her. She blames herself for not calling Jennifer often enough or realising anything was wrong. But with four kids under six, she has her hands full. Mind you, if her sister had asked, I've no doubt Anna would've done anything to help.'

Reeve screwed up her mouth, emphasising the juts of her facial bones. She'd lost a few kilograms too many since joining their team. Stress, long hours, and skipped meals had done the same to Sturt over her time with the homicide squad, and with a wash of guilt she acknowledged that she hadn't been looking out for Reeve.

'Jennifer's parents, Geoff and Margaret Locke, reckon she never mentioned visiting Anna to them, either. And apparently, they expected the Denton family for lunch on 16 May, but they didn't turn up. The Lockes insist Jennifer would've called if her plans had changed and she wouldn't leave her son behind for a daytrip, let alone an extended stay. *In fact*, none of these witnesses can recall the last time Jennifer went anywhere outside of Melbourne without Martin and both kids.'

Sturt referred to the file. 'So, mum and dad reported Jennifer and Heidi missing on 18 May?'

'Uh-huh. But the desk sarge assumed it was all a

misunderstanding and that Mrs Locke had overreacted, so he didn't pursue it. In desperation, Mr Locke contacted a friend-of-a-friend stationed at Prahran on 21 May, and eventually, the case made its way to Connolly's unit.'

Sturt took one mouthful of her juice and couldn't stop glugging, so she waved her junior on. She hadn't realised how dehydrated and hungry she'd become, and the meal, courtesy of Reeve, barely made a dent on it.

'Anyway, Prahran had hubby in, made general inquiries, hit a brick wall and–' Reeve broke off to answer the telephone, listened, and handed the receiver across. 'Connolly, boss.'

'Howdy.'

'Progress, Rose?'

The peal of her mobile phone distracted Sturt but she let the call go to message bank. 'Not yet, mate. Jude's done some prelims, and we're going over the file.'

'Martin Denton is a rum one,' Connolly said. *'Comes across distraught and I can't prove he's culpable of anything apart from wasting our time with all these stories—yet—but my gut's screaming that the wife and child have come to grief at his hands.'*

Sturt's shoulder blade buzzed. The old knife wound did that when *her* gut tried to talk. It clearly agreed with her mate from the Missing Persons Unit.

After they'd wrapped up and disconnected, she checked with Reeve, 'So far Denton's changed his story three times?'

'Four. First, Jennifer had gone to visit her sis.' Reeve talked and paced. 'When the family disputed that idea, he said they'd misunderstood him, she was visiting a girlfriend. Then, he spun a story about a stalker, alluding to her abduction. Latest is a confession that Jennifer discovered she was pregnant again, which triggered a nervous breakdown and caused her to take off.'

'Pretty elaborate.' Sturt exhaled loudly through her nostrils.

'And doubtful. Connolly hasn't been able to substantiate the breakdown theory. Although Jennifer wasn't,' Reeve corrected her slip, *'isn't* one for girls' nights, and her friends are largely from Heidi's three-year-old kinder group and Shawn's school, she's seemingly very well liked and a devoted mum.'

'What doting mum would leave her seven-year-old son without explanation or goodbye?'

'Exactly.' Reeve stopped pacing to pick up Sturt's photograph of the young family. She mumbled, 'Heidi's the spitting image of her mum.'

She looked shocked when Sturt lost it and thumped the desk.

'Hell, I hate these cases, Jude. Adults can make their own beds. But kids…it's so bloody wrong. What could Heidi have done to deserve this? Or the baby? Assuming Jennifer is pregnant. Jesus, I should've been a bloody teacher like my dad wanted!'

Reeve slowly pulled her eyes away from her boss and stared at the photograph again.

Sturt wondered if Reeve's mind played the same trick that hers did. Their jobs hinged on violent death but cases like this were her worst nightmare. They got right under her skin. When she'd looked at that photo, after a few moments she hadn't seen the little Heidi Denton as pictured – a round-faced imp with messy brown hair, huge liquid-chocolate eyes, cheeky grin. Instead, the image transformed into the child with torn clothes, bruised and bloody, dead.

Reeve finally asked, 'Really, boss? Reckon you had a choice?'

Her smoky-grey eyes widened, but her tone said everything. Reeve had always planned to be a detective, and once she'd achieved a post with a crime investigation unit, she'd raised the stakes. She'd made an appointment to see Sturt, sat where she was today and announced she'd wait as

ON THE JOB

long as necessary to achieve a post in the homicide squad. Four years later, she'd knocked back a promotion to sergeant but gotten her wish.

Truth be told, Sturt herself had been known to say she couldn't imagine doing anything else, despite the brutality and bureaucracy. So, she replied, 'Hell no. My grandpa was a cop; my dad wanted me to teach. Trouble was I spent all my energy "solving" whatever hit the news... Tell you what, though, a couple of years in the job cured my idealism about making a difference. We don't make a bloody difference. We just improve the commissioner's clearance rates.'

'Bit cynical, isn't it?'

Sturt shook her head, then admitted, 'Yes and no.' She didn't elaborate. They both knew her cynicism stemmed from the irreversible violence they dealt with, day-in-day-out. They couldn't bring back the dead. On the flipside, she liked to think they made a difference to the victims' loved ones and *just maybe* protected the wider community by putting away brutal perps.

Reeve backtracked. 'So, do we believe Denton – that Jennifer's pregnant?'

'There's usually some truth in every lie. If it's early days, it'd explain why she hadn't seen her obstetrician.'

'But wouldn't Denton have sought help if she was close to a nervous breakdown?'

'You'd think, wouldn't you?'

With that, Sturt turned her attention to updates from her other crews, and Reeve arranged an interview with Jennifer's son Shawn, and parents. They would come in together, as Geoff and Margaret Locke had been caring for their grandson since late-May. Reeve then worked the phones, verifying information supplied by Missing Persons, until they arrived.

To make the process less intimidating for the child and grandparents, they gathered in Sturt's office and both detectives wore shirts without their suit jackets. While Reeve offered Shawn jelly beans from a jar on the desk, Sturt observed the boy. He bore an even stronger resemblance to his father than photos revealed.

As Shawn sorted his lollies into coloured groups, he relaxed into the sofa where he perched between his grandparents. Conversely, the Lockes grew more restless, obviously fearful of the worst from the summons to the St Kilda Road Police Complex.

Sturt lifted her palms, aiming to reassure them. 'Senior Sergeant Connolly has asked for fresh eyes on the disappearance of your daughter and granddaughter. We often combine resources on Missing Persons investigations, so please don't read anything sinister into my unit's involvement.'

Reeve would have explained all that on the phone, yet Geoff Locke's forehead smoothed fractionally. The inspector then asked the older couple to help her build a picture of the family.

The Lockes constructed an image of the perfect nuclear family: a wife and homemaker, two delightful children, a husband who was a good provider, respected by his parents-in-law. They said the family lived in its own home in one of Melbourne's growth suburbs. Despite the hefty mortgage for the purchase and renovations, they managed on Denton's sole wage, as he and Jennifer valued stay-at-home parenting.

'And that's why we don't believe for a minute that Jen forgot our lunch plans for the sixteenth of May.' Margaret tugged a hankie out from her sleeve. She worried the lacy edges until Sturt thought she'd shred the fabric onto the floor.

Little Shawn picked up the tension from his grandmother. He swung his legs, banging his shoes against the sofa. The grandfather put his arm around the boy.

The detectives didn't push to fill the gap and eventually Margaret spoke again. 'Our daughter has good old-fashioned values. She'd never leave her husband and son voluntarily, even more so if she's expecting again.'

Sturt saw the older couple's distress notch up. Fortunately, Shawn had tuned out and wandered over to her bookshelf.

She leaned close, her gaze pinned on Jennifer's parents, but Reeve beat her to it, gently asking, 'You were surprised to hear she's pregnant?'

Geoff made a whistling gasp. 'Stunned.' He sounded pained. 'We were first to know when our Jen fell with Shawn and Heidi.'

Then, while the little tacker was engrossed in a bunch of photos, Sturt asked the vital question. 'What are your feelings as to Jennifer and Heidi's whereabouts?'

'Stranger,' Margaret answered immediately. 'A stranger took them.' She gestured to her grandson and halted, but the terror in her and her husband's eyes spoke volumes. They believed their daughter and granddaughter were dead.

They took a coffee break, Reeve popping out for a banana milkshake for the little boy, and subsequently the Lockes were more composed.

On Sturt's nod, Reeve chatted with Shawn about his family. He painted a similar picture of a tight-knit, happy household.

'You're doing a top job there, little man.' Sturt offered the boy another dip into the lolly jar.

Then Shawn gave them the first break in the case. 'Daddy was really mad at Mummy before she went away.'

Sturt's pulse tap-danced. Finally, they had something greater than instinct, alongside his inconsistent stories, that indicated Martin Denton was behind the disappearances. But when they probed his statement, the boy became tearful.

His grandmother hugged him, begging, 'Tell the police ladies whatever you can remember that might help them find Mummy and Heidi, sweetie.'

He nodded more gravely than any seven-year-old should.

'Mummy's friend Danny had been to our place and Daddy didn't like it.'

'Danny?'

'He means Daniel Burns,' Margaret explained. 'He and Jen dated as teenagers and they're still very close.'

Geoff interrupted. 'There's no hanky-panky between them, mark my words.'

Reeve sussed out Shawn's impressions, while Sturt considered the information objectively. The boy described a platonic relationship. But the lead provided a motive for Denton—whether or not his powerful jealousy was justified—and it further involved Burns as a witness or suspect.

After the family departed, Reeve gathered information on Daniel Burns, while Sturt worked through tedious budget reports until interrupted by a call from Connolly.

'We've got something from hubby's appeal.'

He sounded excited. And as he clearly referred to an appeal Denton made for the return of his wife and daughter, Sturt demanded, *'What* something?'

'A Tamara Schmidt called Crime Stoppers. She's a family counsellor that Jennifer's been seeing.'

'And?'

'Well, all this is off the record, but Jennifer's been troubled by a clandestine affair she's been conducting for the past year or so.'

Sturt whistled. 'How troubled?'

'Pretty damn worried, especially because her baby is lover boy's.'

Eyebrows hiked, Sturt asked, 'Does Schmidt know the lover's name?'

'Unfortunately, not. Although she did add that Jennifer said her boyfriend wouldn't be happy about the pregnancy and she didn't know what to do. Apparently, an abortion wasn't an option, but living with hubby while carrying another man's child didn't sit with her either.'

An adrenaline rush replaced Sturt's deep-set fatigue. Schmidt's statement strengthened motives for Denton and

Burns. Equally, it gave some credence to the further possibility that Jennifer had absconded. Still pondering, she described the interview with the Lockes and Shawn to Connolly, then summoned Reeve.

The younger detective had discovered noteworthy information, too. Burns had form for his involvement in a student protest back in '91, various minor traffic infringements and an altercation with a man in a nightclub two years ago. Burns was no 'Chopper' Read but he had a history of low-level violence, coupled with reason to be angry: his girlfriend's unwanted pregnancy...*if* he was Jennifer's lover.

Senior Sergeant Dinkerton entered Sturt's office. As the three conferred on another case, Sturt's mobile phone rang out, then Reeve's. The latter call transferred to message bank before the impromptu meeting concluded.

Reeve checked her new message. She stared at the small screen for so long, that Sturt wondered if she'd received bad news.

Eventually, Reeve turned to her and said, 'Ring Baz. He's tried texting and ringing you. You're in the shit.'

Sturt slapped her forehead. She'd forgotten to return her hubby's calls.

'Meanwhile, *I'm* getting Denton's phone records.' A smile spread over Reeve's face. 'We need to take another look. I think we've got him!'

Recalling the man at the last appeal—his appearance just too immaculate, his tone and brown-eyed gaze just too earnest, everything about him just a fraction too doleful and charismatic to be true—Sturt's heart beat out of rhythm.

Minutes later, they spread the telephone records across Sturt's desk and studied the landline and mobile phone traffic for the weeks around Jennifer's disappearance.

'Right, frequent quick calls from the landline to Denton's mobile and some from his mobile to her mobile, as well as the landline. It's almost as though she had to check in at certain times of the day.'

Sturt shook her head, impressed by Reeve's jump from Baz's missed calls to Jennifer's patterned behaviour.

'But there's no traffic between the landline or Denton's phone and Jennifer's mobile after 13 May, the day that Shelley Simpson reportedly saw Jennifer and Heidi...*because* Denton knew it was pointless calling his wife after he'd killed her. If he really thought she was missing—for whatever reason—he would've constantly tried to contact her.' Reeve waved her hand. 'Look at good old Baz. Your hubby wants to speak with you, but you don't answer your phone. So, he has to send me an SMS, to put a bomb under you to call him back. The point is: *he keeps trying*.' She hesitated and chewed her bottom lip, her thinking habit. 'But why do you reckon Denton killed his wife and daughter, but not their son?'

'I don't know. Who knows how these scumbags think, Jude? Boy-child, he's more like his dad than his mum, whereas Heidi's the opposite. Maybe Denton's suspicious as to whether she's his.' Sturt tapped her blunt fingernails on the desk. 'Let's get him and Burns in.'

Reeve's answer was lost in a massive yawn. Sturt could've counted all her fillings, not that she had many.

'Organise it for tomorrow. Get Burns here first thing and Denton around lunchtime if you can. Connolly will want to sit in on the interview with Denton, if not both.'

Reeve nodded and moved to make the calls.

'When you've done that, Jude, go home and rest. Do not pass go.'

'And *you*,' Reeve pointed, 'go kiss and make up with Baz.'

Sturt saluted and followed orders.

Midway through the next day they faced Martin Denton across a plain square table. They had dealt with Burns earlier and what he'd told them made Sturt carefully blank her expression. Connolly entered the stark chamber last, activated the illuminable 'Interview in progress' panel and slammed the soundproof door. He stood behind Denton.

Sturt pinned their suspect with her eyes. He smoothed the lapels on his jacket, then gave her a smile. So out of place that it made her gut knot.

After Reeve addressed the formalities for the recording, Connolly launched their strategic attack. 'Lost a bit of weight, Martin.'

The man turned to the Missing Persons officer behind him.

Reeve said, 'It must be hard all on your own. It's been nine weeks now. How are you coping?'

She sounded concerned but again Denton didn't answer. He shot a nervous glance at his solicitor.

Sturt's voice made the suspect turn to her. 'Miss them, do you, Mr Denton?'

He cleared his throat and admitted missing his wife and daughter.

Sturt dropped the faux sympathy. 'Regret it, Denton?'

'Regret what?' he replied in falsetto.

'*Well*,' Connolly said, causing the man to spin around again. 'How about the emotional abuse of your wife for the past eight years?'

Burns had supplied that gem to them a few hours earlier.

Reeve added, 'Or the murder of your daughter? Assuming that Heidi was your child. Of course, Jennifer's unborn baby wasn't.'

The left nostril of Denton's solicitor twitched. He cautioned his client.

'Perhaps the only thing you regret is letting your wife take up with her old flame.' Reeve leaned forward and adopted a conspiratorial tone. 'Danny Burns is quite a honey, actually. *Gorgeous* eyes. You know, they're similar to Heidi's in colour.'

Red discs burned on Denton's cheeks.

Sturt said, 'Very smart withdrawing the cash from the ATM using Jennifer's card, by the way. If you'd ticked just one more box, you might've got away with it. The thing you forgot was the phone calls.'

Denton stretched his neck forward in unspoken query.

'You forgot to fake telephone calls between you and Jennifer. In all those nine weeks that your wife's been missing, you've not left one message on her mobile. Yet, you were distraught. You implored her abductors to release her. Then, you begged her to come home, after spinning the story that she'd had a nervous breakdown and run away. Come on, mate, you used to touch base at least five times a day.' Reeve's tone was caustic. 'And you haven't tried to call her *once* since she disappeared.'

Denton's solicitor rose and gathered his gear.

'Sit down,' Reeve snapped. 'Your client's not going anywhere.'

'Not until we've charged him with the murder of his wife and *three-year-old* daughter.' Connolly's stress upon Heidi's age highlighted the heinous breach of the duty of care by father to daughter.

Denton covered his face with shaky hands. His solicitor's deadpan expression slipped for a second as he returned to his seat.

The three detectives pummelled Denton without pausing.

'When did you learn of your wife's affair with Daniel Burns?'

'When did you discover your wife was carrying his child?'

'When did you start to question if Heidi was your daughter?'

'I put it to you, sir,' this came from Sturt, 'that you murdered Jennifer and Heidi Denton on or about 13 May this year. I further put it to you that you caused the termination of Jennifer Denton's pregnancy during this act. Do you understand, sir, that this, too, is a crime?'

A sob escaped from Denton. His hands still hid his face.

'Mr Denton,' Reeve said. 'Detective Inspector Sturt asked if you understand what you have done.'

Denton mumbled incoherently.

'Speak up for the recording, sir.'

The solicitor laid a hand on his client's shoulder and murmured into his ear. Denton uncovered his face and placed his palms on the table. He shrugged off his counsel and looked directly at Reeve.

'Gone,' he said. 'My little problems are all gone now.'

The hairs on Sturt's forearms prickled.

'Gone away.'

After ninety seconds of silence, Connolly spoke. 'Where have they gone?'

Another sixty seconds elapsed.

Reeve asked, 'Did you kill Jennifer and Heidi?'

'Oh yes,' Denton replied. He sounded happy. 'It was easy. You see, they were all asleep. I hit Jennifer with Shawn's cricket bat, across the back of her head. She made a kind of *uwfugh* noise, but it wasn't very loud. I only had to hit her a couple more times,' he pointed to his temples and the base of his skull, 'then it was all over.'

'What did you do then, Mr Denton?'

'Went to sleep,' was his matter-of-fact reply.

Hell. He slept with the body of his wife nearby – though surely not in the same bed. Sturt made a note to follow up that detail later.

Reeve must've thought likewise, as she pushed the chronology along. 'What did you do after you woke up?'

'I gave the children their breakfast and took Shawn to school. The girl grizzled for her mother. So, I took her to Jennifer. The pillow made her quiet.'

The bastard smothered his little girl. Sturt sensed a change in Reeve's posture and swivelled her eyes. She realised her junior was peripherally watching *her*, or more accurately, her hands, which were balled on the tabletop. She dropped them to her lap, still clenched. She'd love to belt the crap out of Denton.

'Did you suffocate Heidi with a pillow?'

The man's eyes flicked sideways at his solicitor, then over the faces of the homicide detectives. 'Yes.'

'Where are Jennifer and Heidi now?'

'I cut them up with the hedge trimmer.'

Shit, you'd think he was talking about cutting a sandwich.

'It didn't work very well through here.' Denton indicated his torso. 'So, I used the circular saw. Put the stuff in the wheelie bin. Problem solved.'

A red-hot poker burned from Sturt's gut to throat. How could Denton be so blasé about the killings? She looked away from the sociopath to her mate, Connolly, whose face was a collage of emotions that the seasoned copper normally kept guarded. Sturt dared not glance at Reeve. She suspended the interview. If she stayed in the room for a second longer, she might stuff everything up by assaulting the heartless bastard.

As the detectives entered Sturt's office, Connolly fisted the air. 'We've got him.'

Sturt couldn't match his joy and judging by Reeve's pale face, neither could she. 'Yep. Now we just have to tell the family and find the remains at the tip.'

'Thanks, boss,' Reeve said. 'I really needed that visual.'

Connolly slumped onto the visitor's sofa and held his head in his hands.

'Danny Burns will be shattered,' Sturt blurted out.

'He will,' Reeve agreed. 'I believed him when he said he hadn't planned on having a baby, but after he came around to the idea, he couldn't wait to start a new life with Jennifer and the kids.'

'We all did.'

Connolly said, 'Thought he confirmed that Heidi wasn't his daughter?'

'He did. But Denton obviously has doubts, doesn't he?' Reeve managed a half-smile.

'Poor Shawn,' Sturt muttered. The little boy had been at the forefront of her mind since Denton had calmly described the dismemberment of Jennifer and Heidi. What a horrific legacy.

She pushed back from her desk and rose. 'Okay, shall we get this over with? Finish off the interview and charge him.'

Connolly opened the door, but Reeve remained seated.

'You don't think it seems too easy?'

Sturt glared at her. 'Nothing about this case is easy.'

'This guy's a pathological liar, right?'

The absolute exhaustion of yesterday returned and Sturt had to lean on her desk.

'He has no heart or conscience and seems to enjoy playing games.' Reeve chewed her lip.

Sturt tilted her head, intrigued.

'He went all shifty with his eyes when I asked if he'd suffocated Heidi.'

She was right.

'I'm not convinced the game's over.'

Horror and wonder hit Sturt. She and Connolly gaped at the younger detective.

'You think Heidi's alive?'

'Holy shit,' Connolly exclaimed.

Sturt started for the door.

Reeve stopped her. 'He won't tell us. He's the game master. He *wanted* to tell us about Jennifer. He let us think he'd killed his daughter, too. But I reckon his ultimate plan–'

Sturt finished for her, 'Is to let Heidi die while we figure it all out.'

The fatigue and hopelessness dissolved. Here was a

chance to help the shattered family that meant a million times more than a conviction and prison sentence. She imagined little Heidi as she'd been in the photo with her mum and brother: happy and healthy.

'Jude, you deserve my job.'

Reeve grinned.

Sturt hadn't seen her do that for a while, but chuckled as she added, 'When I retire.' She plugged an internal number into the phone. 'Dinkerton. Can you get whoever's available into the briefing room in thirty? Good.'

Within two hours, they'd charged and remanded Denton, hoping they could downgrade one of the murder counts to kidnap, unlawful imprisonment, and/or attempted murder when they found Heidi. They'd mounted a massive search at the tip that serviced Denton's neighbourhood thanks to recruits from the academy and as many uniformed officers that could be spared. The Lockes and Danny Burns were en route to St Kilda Road for further interview. Several homicide detectives were meeting with associates of Martin Denton, friends of his wife and their neighbours. And Reeve continued to troll through the records because so far it appeared that their suspect had no blood kin, apart from Shawn, and no one who called him a mate, despite his superficial charm.

Sturt told the team to keep digging. Someone held the key to where Denton would've secreted his daughter. She barked orders, demanded updates, and made tight notations on a whiteboard. She paced through the office, tearing at the steel wool that had replaced a head of black hair thanks to the job.

Then she halted in mid-stride. 'Connolly! Reeve!'

They came running.

'Game master, huh?' Sturt nodded at her female colleague.

She pulled up a clean whiteboard and waved a blue marker as she talked. 'The game centres on Jennifer.' She wrote 'Jennifer' in the middle of the board, then drew an offshoot to the right and scribbled notes that corresponded with her verbalised thoughts. 'Affair with Danny Burns. Equals unborn baby. "Solved" by her death.' To the left of Jennifer's name, the inspector slashed a fresh line and scrawled, saying, 'Heidi. Denton questions if Burns is her father. Even if not, Burns and the Lockes will be destroyed if Heidi dies slowly through the game.' With a red marker, she circled Danny Burns, then thumped the marker tip against the whiteboard with her next words. 'Burns is Jennifer's ex-boyfriend and current lover. And he was going to steal Denton's wife and family.'

Sturt studied her colleagues. Reeve listened with her palms sandwiched in a prayer pose. Connolly jammed the knuckles of one hand under his nostrils. A bunch of support staff and detectives had joined their huddle, poised like golf spectators while the favourite took a tricky putt. Sturt's old wound buzzed, echoing the expectancy.

'If I were game master and wanted to architect the perfect revenge on my cheating wife and her boyfriend, I'd link it to him somehow – maybe to something about their past... because that's where all the rot began, right?' Sturt drew a vertical line underneath Burns's name, terminating in a question mark. 'We need to know everything about Burns around the time he first dated Jennifer. Why did they break up?'

Reeve answered, 'He failed her ultimatum to cut back his boozing, which he admitted used to screw his headspace and make him a brawler.'

'Okay, he seems to be most open with you, Reeve, so he's yours when he arrives,' Sturt checked her watch, 'which should be in approximately five minutes. Find out about anywhere special to them as a couple in those early days.'

'Because *that's* where he's hidden Heidi,' Connolly said.

'I think so. *Yeah*. I really do.'

They prepared questions for Burns and Jennifer's parents,

while they awaited their respective arrivals. Everyone in the squad room perked up when the receptionist announced that Burns was downstairs.

Reeve escorted him into the witness room. It was less austere than the interview room, yet more formal than one of the offices or the briefing room. On the downside, it didn't have a one-way mirror or microphone, so Connolly and Sturt waited impatiently in the latter's office.

'It's taking too long.'

Connolly rolled his eyes. 'Settle.' Then he went to meet the Lockes, leaving Sturt alone and frustrated.

Frustration turned to panic. They'd had Martin Denton in custody since lunchtime. God knows how long it'd been since the man had checked on Heidi, given her food and water. Was it this morning? Yesterday? Last week?

Are we too late?

Sturt pictured the little girl. As before the image fuzzed into the child's lifeless body and she shook her head to clear her mind.

We can't be.

Reeve burst into her office, beaming so broadly that Sturt knew she'd discovered something. She wanted to hug her.

'His grandpa's property.' Reeve's staccato speech conveyed urgency, maybe excitement too. 'There's an old cottage that used to be the main house. It became rundown – the family abandoned it and built a bigger one. Denton found out that Jennifer and Danny used to meet there—at the old place—to make out. Rickety these days…but still standing.'

'Where exactly?' Sturt plucked up her phone, ready to rally the locals.

'Shepparton.' Reeve drew a breath and managed, 'About a kilometre from where Jennifer's parents used to live, which is not far from her sister's place.'

She dictated the address and a few minutes later Sturt relayed it down the line to the local station. As much as she'd love to be there if—*when*—they found Heidi, the two-hour commute from Melbourne could cost the girl her life.

Then there was nothing to do but wait. The tension in the squad room was palpable. People snapped instead of speaking. They snatched up phones on the first ring and slammed them down after they'd cursorily dealt with the unwanted call. Sturt's stomach churned and burned. She couldn't eat or drink. One of the team came in with a hot dog and the smell nearly made her throw up. Reeve and Connolly didn't seem to fare better.

Her guts plummeted when her mobile rang. She pulled it out and answered. 'Rose Sturt, homicide squad.'

'Sergeant Tomms, Shepparton.' Without further ado, the bloke added, *'We found her.'*

His tone gave away nothing and Sturt held her breath.

Tomms said, *'Heidi's alive! She's off to hospital, but she'll be okay.'*

'She's alive!' Sturt echoed and whooped.

The room erupted. A good day in their office was nailing a killer. Today, they'd also helped save a life.

Connolly scooped up Reeve and swung her around. She laughed and accepted high-fives from the team. Workmates slapped Sturt's back while she spoke to Tomms. Half her brain stayed in the moment. The other half saw three-year-old Heidi break into an infectious grin and flourish a double thumbs-up.

THE JOB V

Move to the country to run a one-cop station
Goodbye rat race
hello the good life
at least for a while
It'll be all about community
handling things not ordinarily part of a copper's domain
Getting to know each and every character in town
not just the troublesome few
Better for the family
clean air, outdoorsy, safe streets, more time together
Because crime is soft—slow—in the country
So they say

SILK VERSUS SIERRA

Winner Scarlet Stiletto Awards 2013
Best Investigative Prize

First published in *Scarlet Stiletto: The Fifth Cut – 2013*

SILK VERSUS SIERRA

'Shit,' she cursed when her hip vibrated. 'Not now.'
Nearly all the 450 permanent residents in town had her mobile number—and hubby Steve's, too—but they never rang on Wednesdays simply to chat. Barb's rest days were no-fly zones except in emergencies, doubly so during karaoke every second week.

She took the call outside. A minute later, she rushed in.
'Babysitter?'
'Work.'
Steve screwed up his nose. 'Take the car. I'll grab a lift if you don't make it back.'
'Wait up for me.' Barb kissed him full-lipped. 'We're definitely having our nookie while the kids are at Sal's.'
'You betcha, babe.'
She drove away feeling a cocktail of emotion. A dash of disappointment at missing karaoke and the chance to defend her title of Loch Sport Gumboot-throwing Champion later—if anyone was dumb enough to take her on—topped with apprehension, excitement, and curiosity.

By the time she had raced home to don her uniform, switched the family sedan for the marked four-wheel drive, and finally nosed the truck down Seacombe Road, eight or nine precious minutes were lost. Compared to a forty-to-sixty-minute response time from other available units, this was speedy. Still, she chafed at the delay.

She trusted her information implicitly. Not much went past certain characters in this town. In fact, the same old fella who'd called in tonight's warehouse alarm had been her first customer here in Loch Sport. Her transfer came through quicker than the sale of their house in Mitcham, so she'd torn herself away from Steve and the kids—only three girls back then—amid a gratifying amount of tears from them, and bucketloads of her own, travelled half-way across the state with one suitcase and a few boxes, and started their family's sea change alone. She'd been unpacking and answered a rap at the door.

A short, leathered bloke with baby's fluff hair stared at her.

'Len Brown,' he announced. 'Just to let you know, this is the police house you've broken into. The police're on their way.'

She'd barked out a surprised laugh and asked him to cancel his call. He did, after she'd proved she actually was their new Officer-in-Charge – aka their only police officer in town.

Now, based on Len's call, she knew an alarm was going silently crazy. Whether it proved to be a non-event or break-in, she'd ascertain in roughly one minute. As it'd already cost her the chance to sing Billy Idol's *White Wedding*, she somewhat hoped for the latter.

Barb slowed after the golf course and pulled right onto Progress Road. The truck's tyres scrunched on sand blown from the road verge. The town's industrial estate consisted of two handfuls of large blocks bound by high cyclone wire fences, a deterrent against 'roos rather than burglars. Several properties were perpetually for sale, as was about a third of the town. Between faded 'For Sale' signs, vacant land and junk strewn across the yards of tin sheds just as neglected, the street wore an abandoned appearance. And set among all this were a few structures that Barb suspected acted as registered addresses for dodgy companies.

Number seven, LS Mining, was one of those on her fishy list. Its silent blue alarm flashed through the darkness. But Barb's eyes were drawn to the steel-grey Commodore on the driveway. Parked at an angle, bonnet to the street, both front doors ajar. It struck her as odd that they'd taken time to reverse in. Or maybe they'd driven out of the shed?

Her mind shifted.

Which first? Check the building or car?

Instinct told her the car. Coppers don't like to enter dark warehouses. Too many mock shootouts at the academy were probably to blame. Besides, the car was closer and might hold the culprits who had set off the alarm.

Barb left the red-and-blue strobes on and took her keys as she exited the truck. Some jokers had taken her vehicle for a spin the one time she'd chanced leaving the keys in the ignition. No harm done on that occasion, except to her pride, but she'd never repeat the mistake.

She extracted the Maglite from her belt and shone it over the vehicle. With boots barely making a sound in the black sand dubbed 'soil', she approached. The sedan's interior light illuminated what appeared to be an empty cabin.

She reached the car, confirmed front and back seats were vacant.

Barb's heartbeat moderated a smidgeon.

Towards the rear quarter on the driver's side she noted a large ding with red paint transfer and a shattered taillight.

She arced the torch as she walked along the passenger side and caught sight of a Transformer toy on the ground about half a metre away. Barb squatted next to it. The Bumblebee autobot looked chewed and knocked about; a twin for her five-year-old Ange's, except for its decapitation. Transformers survive tough love, so it must've taken something like an adult's weight to break it.

Still thinking about the toy, she took in sticky smears on the passenger door trim and crumbs scattered over the seat.

Definite kid territory.

Her stomach flipped. Where was the kid now? Ange would never abandon one of her beloved toys, squashed or not. What'd prevented the kid from rescuing the autobot?

Barb touched the bonnet. Hot. She snatched away her palm.

Another quarter-circle and she swept the torch over the cockpit again, although from the driver's side. The cupholders in the centre console contained a half-empty bag of jelly snakes and Audrey Hepburn sunglasses.

She leaned in to examine dried splotches on the charcoal carpet, then squinted at a stain on the grey leather seat.

Blood?

She straightened. Should she find the boot release and search the storage space? Or skip to the warehouse to ascertain what had happened there and if her car occupants were inside?

A screech made her head rip sideways towards the end of the street, which terminated at the tip entrance. She saw a car fishtail and skew into a fence, caving in ten metres of chain-link wire.

The car shot past so close to the Commodore that the driver's door rocked on its hinges and Barb's shirt flapped against her flank.

Immediately, she retrieved her truck, took pursuit, and called in the chase.

'…in pursuit of red Audi. Euro plate. Victor. Sierra. Lima. Kilo. One. One.'

Barb swiped at sweat that blurred her eyes as she gave D24 particulars of her location.

'Also run a plate-check on an abandoned Commodore. Both are connected with my potential burg at Progress Road. Sierra. Tango. Yankee. Three. Three. Eight.'

All police vehicles were kitted out for officers to run their own checks, but Barb couldn't manage that and a high-speed chase along the Seacombe roadway. The sole road out of town was fairly straight but too rugged for this type of speed. The truck jumped as it hit potholes and Barb gripped the wheel harder.

'…update speed please.'

She glimpsed the speedo. '140.'

Meanwhile, the Audi increased its lead.

Barb compressed the accelerator. Her pulse galloped. The truck was no sports car and she strained to manage it at 165 clicks.

She sent up a silent prayer. *Please God, don't let a 'roo jump out in front of me.*

'ETA on backup?'

'No available units in your vicinity. Minimum fifty-five minutes…'

She hissed out a sigh. *No surprise. I'm on my own.*

A crackle interrupted her thoughts, then: *'…road conditions and current speed?'*

'Clear, dry, just me and the suspect vehicle…'

Dark, potholed, 'roos lurking in the scrub near the road.

'Current speed 170.'

A rattle came from near the tailgate. Barb tensed. At this speed, it wouldn't take much to flip the truck. Her palms dampened.

'Confirm that. Continue to monitor and update. Note, suspect Audi—Victor, Sierra, Lima, Kilo, one, one—registered to Vincent Silk, South Melbourne.'

Barb shook her head and stared through the windscreen at the ever-increasing gap between her and the luxury sedan. So,

VSLK was an acronym of the owner's name. That made his faux Euro plates doubly pretentious.

What brought you from the big smoke to my town, Silk?

The radio crackled again. *'Commodore—Sierra, Tango, Yankee, three, three, eight—registered to TR Auto Repairs, also South Melbourne.'*

Barb pondered on the commercially registered car. It didn't tell her much, except that both vehicles were a long way from home and definitely connected.

'Either vehicle reported stolen?'

'Negative.'

Not stolen, or else the owners hadn't realised yet.

Tell me, Sierra, what are you doing here, along with your mate Silk?

Except that Silk and Sierra weren't mates if the dinged rear-end of the Commodore came courtesy of one red Audi.

The Audi put on another burst and Barb flattened her foot. The speedo shot upwards.

At 210, she radioed through.

'Current speed 210 and suspect vehicle well-ahead. It's unsafe to proceed. I'm calling off the chase.'

She hated doing it, but another vehicle could enter the road from one of the tracks. She couldn't risk it and had Buckley's of catching the car in this heap anyway. The truck suited the more sedate pace of Loch Sport's typical police jobs: drunks, domestics, collisions, community meetings, along with occasional natural and accidental fatalities, firebugs, and wildlife euthanasia duties.

Barb pulled a U-turn. She headed back to deal with the dumped Commodore and warehouse break-in, and radioed through an addendum, a KALOF requesting local units 'keep a lookout for' the Audi.

Next, she speed-dialled a number on her phone.

'On your way home, babe?'

'It could be a long one, darl.'

'Anything I can do?'

'Keep that twinkle in your eye for later.'

She heard Steve's chuckle as they disconnected.

Barb left on bells and whistles while she returned to Progress Road at a safer speed. The truck's headlights cut through the darkness as she cornered and flicked off the siren. She braked at the spot she'd parked earlier. The blue light outside the building still pulsed.

All was the same as before, without one vital item: the grey Commodore.

Barb jumped down from the truck and slammed the door. The sound cracked in the night and a startled mob of 'roos bound away to feed elsewhere.

A flash of the torch revealed the beheaded Transformer and near it, some fresh scuffs in the sandy dirt, but no clue as to the whereabouts of the car.

Barb straightened and pinned her eyes on number seven. At least she could deal with that alarm.

Easily said, yet every sense worked overtime as she edged towards the shed. Her left hand operated the Maglite, her dominant right was free, and she used it to push the access door open wide enough to slip through. The same hand reverted to hover over her service weapon.

'Police. Anyone here?'

She strained but heard nothing.

At the luminous panel near the entrance, Barb checked her notebook and plugged in four digits. The screen flashed to 'alarm off'.

In this isolated district, private security and/or Barb attended emergencies such as tonight's and the non-resident owners of LS Mining had entrusted her with key and alarm code rather than old Snowy in his battered panel van. She'd met a petite bottle-blonde there once, purportedly one of the directors, for the code and key handover. Right now, she couldn't recall much about the woman except that she'd been overdressed for the remote beach town, wearing a white pants suit and blingy sunglasses.

Until now, Barb hadn't been inside this place. She'd always held suspicions about what, if anything, went on here, particularly when Blondie gave her a Melbourne business-hours-only emergency contact number.

Apparently, her intuition hadn't corroded from six years of one-member station policing. A flick of the switch shunted the tin shed into bright light. It was an empty shell, cobwebbed and dusty. Curtains over the tiny window stunk of mildew. The place looked undisturbed for years, except for two parallel stripes through the dust on the concrete floor and a greasy oil patch between them.

Barb strained her eyes. She squatted and scanned. *Make that two tyre tracks, an oil patch, and a bunch of shoeprints.* Several were pint-sized prints, which made her anxious.

She mentally listed everything since her first arrival at the warehouse and jumped when her portable radio squawked with an update on her KALOF.

'...*Rosedale and Sale units report zero sighting of suspect Audi.*'

She shrugged. Silk could've headed towards Seaspray rather than taking the Longford route or maybe he was yet to come into range of the other cars.

Or he's doubled back.

She shivered despite the muggy night.

Her mind twisted to the vanished Commodore, perhaps with an injured driver and child in the midst of all this, and Barb felt a stir of urgency less common these days than during her previous suburban postings. Whatever was going down, she wanted it sorted fast and without casualties.

After she'd secured the building, she added the Commodore to the KALOF, then dug out her mobile and dashed to the police truck.

'Steve,' she said, when her hubby picked up. 'Keep an eye

out for two out-of-town cars – a steel-grey Commodore around a 2004 model and a new red Audi. Both are sedans.' She quoted the rego numbers and added, 'Let me know if you see either but *don't* get involved. The occupants could be dangerous or in danger, I don't know which.'

She called off after assuring him she'd be careful and made a succession of similar requests to the CFA captain Snowy, Bev at the Seafarer Hotel, and Len. The small-town grapevine would do the rest and soon hundreds of extra eyes would be on the lookout.

After she'd turned over the truck engine, Barb hesitated. The blood and sticky food crumbs in Sierra's car had her worried.

Sweat puddled between her boobs. Uneasy and pumped, her nerves buzzed. She tamped down the emotions and reasoned through the case.

Somehow, Sierra knew the LS Mining shed was unoccupied. However, any local could've guessed that and passed it on. What puzzled her more was that someone —*Sierra?*—triggered the alarm *after* they'd been parked inside the building. That didn't make sense. Unless, say, they'd deliberately set it off to enlist help.

Her help.

Think. Fast!

The truck's motor vibrated through the steering wheel. Barb itched to plant her foot but forced herself to pause and process the situation.

She presumed Sierra was on the run with a young kid and came here for refuge. And that was after Sierra sustained an injury and bled on the carpet and seat. Silk/the driver of the Audi somehow followed-slash-found them here and at some stage the cars clashed. Sierra and child were hiding when Barb arrived, and Silk took off in a hurry but could be on his way back.

Barb's brow puckered and she shook her head.

An elaborate scenario, but is it pure fiction?

She flicked her thumbnail against her front teeth.

Tap, tap.

Her next headshake was decisive. Both Mum and Cop radars combined into certainty. She couldn't explain or dismiss it. If she wasn't spot on, she'd struck bloody close.

Now, she drove. Barb turned left towards town because the other option overwhelmed her. Numerous tracks came off Seacombe Road and a lone cop couldn't quickly inspect them all.

She followed Lake Victoria at a slow pace and scanned continuously. Meanwhile, a follow-up plate check on both vehicles revealed neither reported stolen so far.

As she crawled through town, it crossed her mind that Sierra mightn't be a thief or connected with the auto repair shop. She (*she? – yes, remember the Audrey Hepburn sunnies*) may have borrowed a friend's vehicle to get away from Silk.

That'd explain the lack of booster seat for the kid.

Could this be a case of domestic violence? An ugly custody dispute?

Frequently the basic theory was spot-on. Like that double-homicide in Natte Yallock where the killer was allegedly the son of one of the victims and motivated by money. It was a tragedy, yet a too-common scenario.

Barb noted curtains twitch as she moved along Victoria Street. She cut across to National Park Road and near the swamp, hooked around onto Toorak Avenue to again hug the Lake Victoria side. It'd be unlikely that Sierra or Silk would stay on the more conspicuous main drag that dissected town.

A couple of fellas from the CFA stood on the nature strip ahead. She pulled abreast and dropped her window.

'I said keep a lookout but don't be too obvious or get involved. Ring me if you see something.'

She shooed them back to their truck and they chuckled yet complied.

Barb swatted a mozzie, then another. But she did it unconsciously. Her mind was fixated on the tango between Sierra and Silk.

She wouldn't abide an outcome similar to the Natte Yallock case.

'Shit. Idiot.'

She reached for her phone.

Her hubby wasn't just a full-time Mr Mum. He was also a home-based IT whiz.

'Can you run a search on LS Mining?'

'Hi honey, I missed you too,' Steve retorted.

'Sorry, darl.' *Thank God we don't have to sweet-talk D24.* 'Same. Now, can you look at the directors and their addresses...please?'

She heard Steve click away, punctuated by rustle sounds from his shirt against the receiver. Soon he said, *'Two directors. Vincent Silk.'*

Of course it is.

He quoted a South Melbourne address. *'And Juliet–'*

'Shit, that's it.' Barb thumped her forehead.

'What's it?'

'Blondie was a Juliet, but she never gave her surname.'

'Huh?'

'I'll explain later.'

Now more about the meeting with the woman from LS Mining came back to Barb. Juliet had deftly sidestepped questions and somehow, they'd ended up talking about their kids.

Our four girls and Juliet's boy, who's the same age as little Ange.

Although he still sounded perplexed, Steve confirmed, *'Her surname's Silk too. Same address.'*

'Bloody hell.'

She'd wasted precious time at the warehouse before she'd

called around for help. Anything could've happened in the meantime.

She rang off and resumed her trawl.

Then her phone and radio went berserk. From all over came reports of the Commodore's or Audi's current location.

Except that it was impossible for the Commodore to be in Cliff and Snipe Streets simultaneously, just as the Audi couldn't be near the caravan park while it was supposedly thirty metres ahead of Barb's truck.

In their excitement to help, the locals' imaginations had gone wild. Fortunately, the flurry settled, which allowed Barb to concentrate.

She must back herself. If she lacked the wits to solve situations alone, she'd never have secured what was traditionally a male job – the run of a one-member station in an isolated seaside country town. She'd jumped through hoops to prove her aptitude and the quirky, sleepy place hadn't extinguished her ability, although she'd seemingly surface-rusted in the salty air.

Notwithstanding the invitation to mozzies, she left the window open and edged the truck forward. The wind was up again. Trees and shrubs swayed in a haphazard swirl with loud whooshes and whistles. In the distance, waves crashed on the surf beach.

Barb had to picture herself as Sierra – *Juliet*.

She hypothesised aloud.

'I'm on the run from hubby, Vincent, with our son. I borrowed a friend's car and came here, to our empty shed.

'I hid the car inside, thought we were in the clear, pulled the car out and spotted Vincent's Audi. I dragged my son back to the shed, accidentally squashed his toy, triggered the alarm, and locked us inside. Someone would let the cops know – it's the type of place that things go noticed. But I hoped it'd be sooner than later because Vincent's angry. He hit me earlier and I bled on the car upholstery.'

Barb could smell her own sweat. If she got this wrong, Juliet and her son were in grave danger.

She went back to her reckonings.

'Luckily, Vincent didn't have a key to the shed and a cop arrived before he broke in. We came out when she chased Vincent off.'

And went where?

Barb crossed National Park Road again, into Wallaby Street. The baked-mud-mixed-with-fart smell from Lake Reeve when it dried up over summer struck her, along with a rush of adrenaline.

Steve may be Mr Mum in their household, but Barb was hands-on too. Where would she take their kids to keep them safe?

Somewhere secluded and preferably with a toilet because God knows kids always need to go at the worst possible times.

The National Park would tempt her but its corrugated dirt road and dead-end held less appeal than the surf beach with its slightly better access options.

She steered over the causeway and the crash of surf amplified. Her high beam picked up a squashed bunny on the bitumen. Blood still wet and sticky, the carcass not yet picked over.

Recent roadkill.
Run over by Juliet or Silk?
Maybe.

Barb circled the truck into the beach car park. Her hands tingled when she spotted the grey Commodore parked in the darkest corner. The red Audi angled behind it, obstructing escape.

Barb parked, blocking the Audi, and checked both vehicles before she paused and listened. All she could hear was the pound of surf. But instinctively she knew where they were.

Urgency made her sprint.

She drew her torch. Her booted feet burrowed into loose, deep sand as she ran down the hill. Light from a new moon glistened on the foamy waves on the horizon but her eyes fixed on the three sets of footprints in the wet sand edging the water.

Ragged tracks of mid-sized, pint-sized, and large footprints led into just mid and large treads. She imagined Juliet had snatched up her child and held him as she raced with her husband in pursuit.

Barb clicked the Maglite's high beam and held it overhead. She accelerated, huffing heavily – she preferred Sudoku and fishing to athletics.

Now she heard shouts over the surf. Her light picked up a cluster. Shapes refined as she approached. She saw the petite blonde she recognised as Juliet scuffle with a hulking male. He struck her backhanded and she sprawled.

Barb's 'Stop! Police!' went unheeded.

A tiny boy cowered before the man. His eyes seemed too large for his face, wide with fear and shock.

'If I can't have you and my boy, no one will.'

Barb swallowed bile mixed with the chicken parma she'd had for tea at the RSL. She never understood the mentality that killing someone you loved was better than letting them go.

Silk hoisted his son like a sack of potatoes and spun to the sea. The boy lifted his chin and pierced Barb with ebony eyes. He stretched his fingers towards her and whimpered.

'Stop!' Barb repeated.

Silk half-turned, snarled, then trotted into the lacy threads of retreating breakers.

One glance at Juliet assured Barb she was conscious and safe for now – unlike her son.

'Let him go!'

Silk ignored her.

Barb tried again, wishing she knew the child's name to make her plea more personal. 'Mr Silk! Let your son go!'

He ran on.

Taser and gun were both too risky with a moving target and the child in close proximity.

What should I do?

Silk's long legs plunged through the waves and increased the gap between them.

The boy screamed and a primal mothering reaction overrode cop protocol. Pocketing her torch to free up her hands, Barb roared and charged.

As her boots struck water and sank into the shifting sand, she assessed her rival. Her solidly built 180 cm meant she was no pushover. But she was a head shorter than the broad-shouldered man.

Waves slapped her calves. She knew the sea floor dropped steeply. In a few more steps Silk and his son would submerge and be sucked into the rip. No time to hesitate, she lunged forward.

She grabbed Silk's collar and yanked him down to her height. She clenched a fist. One chance is all she'd get.

Crunch.

Her knuckles connected with his temple. He grunted. His eyes widened, then blanked. His body slackened and the boy splashed into the water.

Barb threw an arm each around the father and son. The little boy struggled.

'It's okay, mate.'

Barb tried to soothe him. But more frightened than ever, he bucked, pitching her into the water. Still clinging to the man and boy, a swallow of seawater made her gag and spit. She managed to drag them onto the beach, then collapsed to the sand. Her lungs burned and salt stung her eyes.

The boy scurried to Juliet, who drew him onto her lap. She

cried loudly, her tears dropping onto his wet curls. The boy clung to his mother and Barb saw his body quake.

Silk lay on the beach. His gaze travelled over his estranged family, then to Barb, who scrambled to her feet, weighed down by her waterlogged uniform. He looked back to mother and son. His fingers spasmed and face contorted. Barb felt a prick of compassion.

Strangely, she heard the last verse of *White Wedding*, the lyrics she would've sung tonight accompanied by the surf.

Nothing fair, all right. Her heart hardened to Silk. *Not safe, either.*

What Silk had attempted in a warped sense of love was the ultimate betrayal of the purest thing in his world: his son.

Barb nudged Silk with her toe, hard. He yelped.

'Too late for regrets.'

His eyes squeezed shut in mute response and she glanced back to the boy. He'd pulled away from his mother to stare at Barb. Saltwater and tears beaded on his face and with his eyes still fixed on her, he crept a thumb into his mouth.

Barb checked on Silk. The fight had gone out of him. If it weren't for his heaving chest, he'd pass for dead. He'd keep for a moment. Yet she angled her body and stayed alert, while she inched towards the child.

'Hiya, little fella. Well done for being very brave.' She gently shook the boy's tiny hand. 'I'm Barb. What's your name?'

He slipped his thumb out just enough to mumble, 'Oliver.'

'Hiya, Oliver.' Barb maintained eye contact with the little boy but directed her next question to his mother. 'Are you both okay for now, Juliet?'

Juliet screamed in the instant that Barb sensed movement behind her. She sidestepped and pivoted a second too late. Silk punched her jaw. Her head snapped back. Her brain rattled as she reeled onto the sand.

She gasped. The bastard had to be stopped.

In a beat, she'd regained her footing, although her eyesight fuzzed. She shook off the sensation, but her reactions were sluggish. She had no hope of stopping Silk from pushing his wife. Juliet flew back and crashed into the shallows of the greedy whitecaps.

Barb was torn. Assist Juliet or protect Oliver and apprehend the husband?

Peripherally, she saw the woman stir, thrash, and crawl to safety. At the same time, Silk grabbed for his son. Oliver's squeal stabbed at Barb's heart. She saw him duck and writhe to avoid his father.

'Stop!'

'Let him go!'

The two women screamed at Silk. His face split into an ugly smirk but his eyes were more chilling. Black pits of spite highlighted by the moon. He snagged Oliver by the collar, although the child struggled.

Juliet sprang from the sand and wrapped her arms around Silk's neck. He flicked her off. Oliver squealed again. Barb launched at Silk, but Juliet somehow beat her and connected a fist into her husband's nose.

'Bitch.'

Silk sliced a hand backwards at Juliet. A sickening snap cut through the sound of the surf. He kicked Barb squarely in the chest and her breath whooshed. She bit the inside of her cheek and tasted blood, then hit the ground, winded again. She took a mouthful of sand, coughed, and spat. Grains crunched between her teeth as she lurched to her feet.

What she saw merged fear into fury.

Silk had sprinted up the beach, making for the ramp to the car park. He held Oliver's hands in one of his own and dragged him. The boy's body bounced and swung. He cried out, a sound of pure terror.

Juliet hauled herself up. She cradled her jaw and swayed, in no shape to pursue her long-legged husband.

Silk had a massive head start and Barb knew she couldn't run him down before he reached his Audi and rammed one or both of the other vehicles. He'd escape with poor Oliver, and God knows what he'd do to the child in a fit of malice.

'Stop him. *Please.*'

But Barb was already in action. She ripped off one steel-cap and staggered in an uneven gait. She blocked the terrible sight of Oliver rebounding behind his father. Extracting the Maglite, she centred it on the back of Silk's head and focused her mind and eye.

'One, two, three…'

The boot flew. She held her breath and followed its sweep. A millisecond after it struck Silk's skull, his knees buckled, and he slumped head first into the sand.

Oliver sprawled next to his father, too frightened—*or hurt?*—to move.

Barb surged onwards. Wet clothes, ten kilograms of equipment belt, and one bootless foot made the distance of forty metres a marathon.

Ten metres away, Silk appeared motionless.

Two metres from his body, Barb spotted what resembled the muscle spasms of roadkill. But she went on high alert. Silk wouldn't get the better of her again.

She landed with a knee to his lumbar. Air burst from his lungs. Barb snapped handcuffs on his wrists, then checked Silk's vitals, and rolled him into the recovery position. Still watchful, she hunched and panted.

Thin arms fastened onto her mid-wheeze. She froze, then inhaled carefully. When that didn't frighten Oliver, she stroked his hands in rhythm with her breathing. With each stroke, his trembling reduced, finally stopping when his mother joined their huddle.

'And that's why you're the reigning gumboot-throwing champion.'

'Steve?'

Her hubby pulled her into a hug. She dug her fingers into his back and inhaled his musky scent.

Then over his shoulder, Barb saw a contingent of townsfolk traipse down the sandy ramp. Wrinkly Ralph, a fisherman who virtually lived on the beach and probably instigated a phone tree, with his mate Len, followed by a motley crew of those born and bred in Loch Sport, alongside sea changers and greenies. Although just a tad slow to arrive, the sight of her weird and wonderful neighbours moistened Barb's eyes. She chuckled and locked lips with Steve.

THE JOB VI

Almost time to hang up the blue monkey suit, trade my Freddy—
police badge to you—for a Senior's Card
Don't mind really – it's been a good life, mostly
Shame my wife isn't here though. Still miss her every day
We'd planned the grey nomad thing, a caravan behind the four-
wheel drive and a never-ending trip around the country
Not sure we would've done it, though—upped sticks and left the
place—not even with a new face, a young bud and his wife, living
in the stationhouse instead of us
Can't now because my girl is long gone. Never thought she'd drop
off first. Lucky the job's kept me busy, my mates and cat filled some
of the hole she left
You know, I might see if Morrie could do with a hand behind the bar
– kill three birds: pull some beers, sort out the rowdy buggers, keep
me busy
Life after the job could grow on me
But before I take to chewing off the nearest ears with tales from the
job, I have to finish The One
Every copper has one. A case that strikes at the defences, feels
personal, gnaws away for as long as it stays unsolved

I've seen what happens when The One drags on, seen the effects of guilt and failure in mates, worse with every month, every year, their obsession wrecking their marriages…or their livers
Not going to happen to me. I will nail the bugger, non-negotiable
Just—somehow—have to beat the clock

WHO KILLED CARLY TELFORD?

WHO KILLED CARLY TELFORD?

At 1.05pm on Thursday 17 November, six adults and a toddler heard a bang that stopped them in their tracks. Only the infant didn't recognise the noise, yet he whimpered, possibly responding to his mother's reaction. And afterwards, the adults all had clear recall of what they'd been doing.

The young mother was cajoling her son to eat mashed banana, which landed on the floor when she abruptly unbent from the highchair. A couple were tending their vegie patch and shock made the hubby cut himself with his trowel. The owner of the general store jumped, and her hand slipped, drawing a line across the 'specials' board. And nearby, the publican heard it as he stacked an empty keg, while his best customer paused with sausage speared on his fork.

Bowles rubbed a hand over his bald head and muttered, 'Hiding in plain sight?' Any copper worth his salt was as suspicious of vivid recall as claims to have heard and seen nothing.

He shrugged, launching from the chair, while Malika shadowed him across the room. A shotgun going off some hundred-odd metres from the pub was extraordinary enough to stick in people's minds.

Stopping at the far wall, Bowles wiggled a finger in his ear as he stared at the photo of the one witness who couldn't speak for herself. She smiled back at him, cheeks popping like shiny pink apples as a calico kitten chewed on her long brown hair. So vibrant, with so much to look forward to.

'We've missed something, Carly. But I'll get the bugger before I retire.' He groaned. 'If only I'd been in Willa that day.'

An ache in his chest reminded him that even if he'd been on the spot, Carly would still be dead. And that, like it or not, the homicide D from Melbourne was right. He'd asked for suspects and Bowles had retorted, 'Has to be an outsider.' His town wasn't squeaky clean, but murder was a far cry from stock theft, drunken aggro, and trespass.

The man in the suit had given the main street a pointed look. 'You've been around in the job, haven't you?' Bowles had nodded. 'So you know people are capable of anything, even in one-horse towns. You're our man on the ground as the local copper. They're *all* suspects at this stage, but who should we focus on?'

After a few weeks, Carly's case had been pushed to the backburner by new deaths on homicide's books. It suited Bowles. He'd been hasty to doubt the detective and to trust his community.

But now it was five weeks on and every day that passed without a significant lead lengthened the odds for cracking the case let alone getting a successful prosecution. And it left him only fourteen days until he hung up the uniform to make it right.

'All we want for Christmas is answers for Carly, hey, Malika?'

It wouldn't feel like Christmas if he didn't uncover the truth and put away her murderer. He'd yet to set up a tree with only a few days to go. The only time he'd missed doing it on the first day of December, a tradition he'd kept going after his wife passed.

He skimmed over the photos he'd tacked to the left, from the mum to the wrinkled pensioner. 'My gut says you're clean and we've dug up nothing at odds with that.'

His gaze shifted to the images of Carly's nearest and dearest. Her shattered parents, Tom and Pam Telford, were people he called friends. He also knew her best girlfriend Christina Halliday, along with the principal of the tiny local school, Johan Petrus. The latter had dated Carly for six months, but that was before her first post in nearby Koura.

Bowles hadn't wanted any of these four to be Carly's killer, but he'd helped to investigate and interrogate them. Her parents were at a doctor's appointment in the city. Colleagues had vouched for both the friend and the old flame. These four had independently agreed that Carly wasn't seeing anyone, Christina adding, 'Carly'd say, "Time for love later."'

She'd been robbed of that, leaving Bowles hungry to nail the person responsible.

'Thank Christ it didn't happen during the folk festival, Carly. One week later and I'd have had twenty-five times more suspects.'

As it was, Bowles had eight – the only adults in Willa that he was unwilling to rule out, each alleging not to have heard the gunshot. Yet at least one of these had: the shooter.

Bowles bent stiffly to scoop up his cat, grimacing at the pain in his old joints. Her whiskers tickled his chin and he chuckled, but the sound died when his throat clenched. Seven years ago, Carly had brought him that spotted kitten in the photo, insisting that he needed the little orphan as much as it needed him. Apparently, missing his wife was admirable but he didn't need to be lonely with it. He had admitted defeat and gave his friend naming rights. She'd come up with Malika. The kitten had grown to a cat that adored Bowles and Carly equally. And now, his constant companion was also a constant reminder of their mutual loss.

She nestled against his chest as he studied the suspects' photos.

First, the neighbour supposedly in bed with the same flu that caused Carly to call in sick. He'd claimed to be feverish, to have heard and seen nothing. Sceptical, Bowles decided the dole bludger wasn't off the hook just because he lacked priors for violence.

Next was a threesome elevated on his list when the wife retracted her alibi, telling Bowles, 'I'm not covering for that SOB.' This led him to link her hubby with another of his suspects, both admitting to fooling around that afternoon. But they'd lied initially, which made them unreliable witnesses. And with the wife's movements now uncorroborated, she couldn't be discounted either.

Malika squirmed out of his tightening grasp. 'Sorry, girl.'

Looking at his remaining possibilities, fatigue crushed Bowles. All the suspects knew Carly—everyone in town did—and although none of the eight owned a registered firearm, he couldn't eliminate them.

'But *why* would they kill her?'

Carly's house was mortgaged and furnished tastefully but inexpensively, and her best friend and parents verified nothing had been stolen when she'd been killed by a single gunshot. She didn't gamble or do drugs and she drank sensibly. By all accounts, she was young, kind, popular, pretty, and smart…

Bowles glanced at the cat by his feet. 'Maybe that's the answer.'

Malika purred.

Maybe poor Carly's only sins were the virtues her killer envied. Scrutinising the photos again, Bowles muttered, 'Which of you is a green-eyed monster?'

Realisation struck a blow to his solar plexus and his gasp was echoed by an anxious meow.

'I'll be back soon.'

Bowles patted the cat before locking up. He ran through his theory as he covered the short distance in the marked car. He wouldn't return without the person who had shot Carly.

Jodi Rice opened the door.

It wasn't the first time that the old copper considered her resemblance to her murdered friend a dubious legacy.

He said, 'Thought you'd like an update.'

Her face registered surprise, wariness, then fell into a grave mask as she nodded. She led him to the kitchen and took out two mugs.

Bowles strolled around the room, waiting until she carried the kettle to the sink before saying, 'Your place is a lot like Carly's, isn't it?'

Jodi's hand hovered over the tap. Then she turned on the water and mumbled, 'Yeah.'

'Replace the cladding outside with weatherboards and they'd match.'

She flicked the kettle switch and shrugged. 'I'm only renting though.'

Bowles mentally logged Carly one-upping Jodi by buying her home. He let silence stretch between them as the water heated and he contemplated what pushed Jodi from coveting Carly's life to taking it.

His certainty escalated as she reached for a coffee canister. Storing the ammunition, he moved to a row of snapshots, an eyebrow raising at Jodi with Willa's school principal, their body language revealing a one-sided attraction. Rejection by Carly's cast-off had to hurt.

Bowles leaned against the fridge and eyed the crest on a folded sheet pinned by magnets. As soon as Jodi turned away, he snatched it and read the section scored by a red-inked cross.

When he lifted his gaze, she was watching him. He had to play this carefully.

'You missed out on the teacher's job at our local next year.'

She gave a sharp nod.

'Carly got it. Hard luck.' Bowles faked sympathy, inwardly cursing the principal who'd said *Carly was the only applicant* when Johan had obviously meant the only *worthy* one.

'Yes.' Jodi sighed. It rumbled with deep weariness.

He pointed to the snapshots. 'Like she got the man you wanted but dumped him later.'

'What did she have that I don't?'

'Nothing,' Bowles lied. 'Yet everyone liked her. She got everything handed to her.'

Jodi didn't speak as she replaced the canister, taking a moment to align it with the others on the shelf.

He said, 'Nice set.'

'Yeah. We—Christina, Carly and I—went into Koura together in the last school holidays, and Carly and I bought a set each.' She smiled softly at the memory.

'Shame about Carly's.'

'Yeah, I nearly cried when they broke.'

'All four of them smashed by the buckshot,' Bowles commiserated, letting the trap snap.

'There were three.' She shook her head, only partly present in the conversation. 'Pity though.'

'I guess in the heat of the moment, you don't think about things like that.'

'No, but she told me she got the job and I–' Jodi froze.

Their eyes met. Her fear as patent as the dots of sweat on her lip.

He prompted her. 'You were so upset and...'

She sighed again, even longer and heavier than before. Silence followed for a few minutes. Bowles watched her almost speak, then change her mind.

'You're tired of all this. Aren't you, Jodi?'

She nodded but remained mute.

'Lie upon lie takes a toll, doesn't it?'

Her chin moved slightly.

Bowles shifted his weight, considering what to say next. He thought he knew what had driven Jodi to kill her long-time friend, but how would he get her to admit it?

'You really did care about Carly, I know that.'

Once again, she acknowledged the statement with a tiny nod.

'You just wanted to be more like her…and then that got out of hand.'

He paused and was only faintly surprised when she spoke.

'I didn't mean to kill her.'

Bowles let the sentence hang for several beats. He had some sympathy for Jodi, wouldn't be surprised if she had a mental health problem, but she'd killed Carly, taking away her future. He wanted her to own that.

'But you took a loaded gun with you.'

Her head drooped.

'You disposed of the evidence. Lied to detectives…to me.'

Her shoulders sagged.

'And you looked her parents in the eye, telling them how sorry you were for their loss and that you hoped the police would find her murderer.'

Jodi's chin jerked up. Her blue eyes were bright with a film of tears. When she sighed this time, the sound hissed with the release of pent-up tension.

'Yes. And now you have.'

Bowles clasped her wrist, and his free hand extracted his handcuffs for possibly the final time, as he stated, 'Jodi Rice, I am arresting you for the murder of Carly Telford…'

PREVIEW OF TELL ME WHY

If you enjoyed *On the Job*, you might also like Sandi Wallace's Georgie Harvey and John Franklin series. Here is a preview from the first instalment *Tell Me Why*.

FRIDAY 12 MARCH

CHAPTER ONE

In her dream, she was still plain and plumpish, her hair streaked with grey. Beyond that, though, everything seemed off-kilter. The first thing she noticed was that she floated above herself as she stood in a paddock. She was without her obligatory glasses and wore a floral housedress, not overalls. The images in her dream distorted and reshaped and became even more unreal. Huge sunflowers covered what would really be their well-trampled top paddock. These flowers grew so abnormally bright that they glowed like miniature suns, and she had to shield her eyes with her hand. The brightness became hot, so hot that she moved a forearm over her face.

Then the cat growled, a long, guttural note that sounded a warning. He nipped her finger and roused her from the dream. More asleep than awake, she soothed him. What had upset the amiable puss?

Her husband shook her. She sat up in bed, puzzled. As she donned her glasses, she saw that he'd pulled on work boots and a woollen jumper over his long pyjamas.

'Quick!' he yelled, shutting their bedroom window.

They reached the front verandah but couldn't see anything for the hedge around the house except an orange flush in the night sky. They could feel the intense heat and hear the sinister sound of uncontrolled flames.

From the picket fence they saw billows of smoke. Several sheds were alight. Her husband sprinted for the hose; she for the telephone, to call the local fire captain.

Panic clutched at her chest while she filled buckets of water. Her knees nearly buckled as she dashed towards the outbuildings.

Which first?

The hay shed was fully involved; a lost cause.

The barn or machinery shed?

No animals in the barn tonight.

The latter, then, as it held the combustibles and expensive equipment.

She dumped the water. It did nothing but sizzle. She ran back to the house, detoured to the water trough and returned with soaked woollen blankets. She crashed into a wall of heat; so fierce it scorched her eyes.

As the hay shed erupted, it sent embers in every direction. She protected her face from those missiles of fire with her arm, mimicking her dream persona.

Wind fanned the roaring tongues, adding to the crescendo.

She coughed as smoke filled her lungs. Fire merged the sweet odours of hay and timber with acrid fumes of fuel, pesticides and rubber. Her eyes watered.

'Where are you?' she cried out to her husband. 'Are you safe?'

She fought the flames harder. She would never give up – on him or the farm.

Above the bellow of the fire and rupturing structures and terrified shrieks of sheep and cattle, she couldn't hear a thing. Throat blistered with heat, smoke and yelling for her husband, she couldn't tell if she managed to make a sound or if the screams were only in her head.

Then, a hand clasped her shoulder and something struck her temple. She crumpled to the ground.

CHAPTER TWO

Senior Constable John Franklin had been cooped up with Paul Wells for hours. Too long without a smoke or coffee because Constable-fast-track-Wells was driving and he didn't pay much attention to those who wore fewer than three stripes on their epaulette.

But that wasn't why Franklin wanted to throttle him. It was because Wells measured time, distance, temperature, power poles and countless other things. Plus he was a rigid perfectionist with as much personality as a dead carp. Franklin's workmates rated the bloke's neurotic traits with fingernails scratching down a blackboard. His two consecutive rest days relegated to distant memories by the OCD freak, he ruled it much worse.

'Four and a half minutes,' Wells said. He tapped his watch.

Franklin groaned. So today's general patrol took five minutes longer than the previous trip – *big deal.*

'Should not have stopped for Charlie Banks…'

And that's the difference between a copper from the country and a cockhead from the big smoke.

Franklin tuned out.

A lonely bugger, poor Charlie often wanted to chew their ears. On this occasion it was about his dog's arthritis, but it was just an excuse for company. Yet Wells evidently thought the schedule more important than a quick chat with the old codger.

Franklin scrutinised the intense constable as he unclipped his seatbelt. The bloke was third-generation cop with dad, uncles and grandfather all among the brass. Odds-on he'd be promoted and back to the city before most coppers learned to scratch themselves. They wouldn't improve him, so somehow they'd have to bide time until he moved on.

Granted, the real problem today wasn't Wells. It came from him. Because he was the single parent of a hormonal teenager with attitude and because after sixteen years in the same country town, he still wore a uniform. He chatted to lonely folk, changed light globes, chopped wood and mowed lawns for elderly widows, pointed the radar for hours on end and sorted out the same drunks, the same domestics. Those were the good days. One of his blackest days had seen him as pallbearer at the funeral of a road victim who was also a mate from the footy club. All a far cry from where he'd planned to be by his mid-thirties.

Some days start badly and end up your worst nightmare. She should have seen the ladder in her new pantihose when she pulled them on this morning—hell, the need to wear a bloody skirt and heels itself—as a damn omen. A sign that she'd end up here, two beers down, stomach clenched while she cursed Narkin.

'Bastard.'

The bartender shot her a glare, not the first for that afternoon.

She hadn't meant to say it aloud and grimaced. She resumed pushing the penne pasta around her plate.

Flight of the Bumblebee pealed. She fished through her bag and frowned at the mobile screen. Number withheld. She thumbed the call switch to answer.

'Georgie Harvey.'

'It's Ruby here.'

Georgie cringed. She had avoided the older woman since yesterday but was caught now.

'Michael and I are hoping you'll look up Susan…'

What was her name? Susan Petticoat, Prenticast? Her neighbour Ruby's supposedly missing friend. Whatever; Georgie wasn't inclined to drive to Hicksville on a wild-goose chase.

She was saved by Ruby's cry of *'You silly duffer! What've you done?'*

The phone clunked. Georgie necked some beer and considered hanging up. She couldn't.

'I'll have to ring back, love.'

The call topped off a crap day. Now she felt guilty about dodging her neighbours to boot.

Disgruntled, Georgie scanned the room. It ought to have been a wood-panelled bar with punters using the pool table, old-timers arguing companionably over the footy, the call of a horse race on the radio; cheerful, noisy and as comfortable as worn slippers. Not this stark, trendy joint, with its white paint, stainless-steel counter, blond-wood seats, piped music and ultra-slick patrons. Even the barman's hair had encountered an oil spill. But this was the closest pub to the courts, and a beer was what she'd needed after her run-in with Narkin.

She speared a mouthful of pasta. It was cold and tasted like spicy cardboard. She pushed the bowl aside.

'Can't smoke in here,' the bartender said.

Georgie glanced at the unlit ciggie between her fingers. She hadn't realised she'd reached for it. She wouldn't have lit up; it was just that beer and smokes fit together perfectly. Pity smoking in pubs had been outlawed. What'd be next, inside people's homes or Melbourne's entire central business district? And was it really a health agenda or simply political?

She flicked her black lighter.

'I wouldn't.' The voice came from behind.

She grinned as Matt Gunnerson slipped onto a stool and held up two fingers with a nod and smile.

'How's crime this week, Matt?' The barman had shot daggers at Georgie since her arrival yet beamed as he greeted Matty.

'It's keeping me out of the dole queue.'

Both men laughed. The barman served two Coronas, and Matty slapped his shoulder in that matey way of his. Georgie marvelled at his easy charm, a handy attribute for an up-and-coming crime reporter. She could do with a dose if she ever cracked a real writing gig, as opposed to scripting and editing boring business resources.

They clinked bottles and swallowed in unison.

Matty commented, 'Didn't go well then, Gee?'

'Have I got *loser* plastered here?' She slashed a line across her forehead.

'Which magistrate did you get?'

'Narkin.'

'Ah.' Matty's sigh summed up fronting Pedantic Percy, as he was dubbed within the legal circle. By reputation he found against self-represented defendants – Murphy's Law, she drew him.

'Ah,' she mimicked. She tapped the file before her and said, 'Laird–'

'Laird's your ex-cop?'

'Yeah. He argued that Pascoe Vale Road's notorious for

metallic reflection distorting radar readings. But their expert rebutted.'

'And Pedantic Percy agreed with theirs?' When she grimaced, he added, 'So you lost. No surprise. You *are* a lead foot.'

'I'm not that bad.'

'Sure…'

'Well, maybe I am,' she conceded. 'Anyway, I copped a fine, plus legals, though I *just* saved my licence.'

'Have you spoken to AJ yet?'

Georgie froze. Adam James Gunnerson, her live-in lover, also happened to be his brother. And he currently ranked high on her taboo list.

She was never happier to hear the *Bumblebee* tune.

While Georgie foraged for her phone, she noticed the sky had clouded over. In the tradition of Melbourne's contrary weather, the beautiful autumn day gyrated to bleak. Pedestrians on William Street scurried for shelter from the downpour or sprinted towards the train station. Except for one woman; she walked on in measured strides, stare fixed on the horizon of skyscrapers, bitumen and traffic lights. It was something Georgie would do.

'It's me again. Ruby.'

Damn. I should've known.

'Michael and I were wondering… Well, will you go to Daylesford for us?'

'I'm sorry, Ruby. Can't talk.'

'What was that about?' Matty asked after she disconnected.

'Nothing.'

Georgie squirmed. She couldn't avoid her neighbours forever. But it was easier to avoid the conversation than turn them down flat.

Just as it was easier to run from AJ's kicked-dog eyes.

Georgie evaded Matty's inquisition by heading for the

cigarette vending machine in the tiny passageway to the toilets. It was one of those days when she'd need more than her ten (or so) Benson & Hedges allowance. She fed the machine a fistful of gold coins and pushed the button.

In the ladies' room, she pulled a brush through her hair, changed her mind and messed it up. She smoothed on lip gloss and examined her reflection in the mirror. She tried a smile, then tweaked her silky black top.

Georgie leaned forward and held up thumb and index finger to make an L on her forehead. Then realised it was backwards. She couldn't even get that right.

Definite loser.

'Um, John. Got a tick?' Tim Lunny said, crooking his finger.

Franklin's stomach flipped. Was he in trouble again? Or worse: about to be permanently rostered on with Wells?

Fuck no, anything but being stuck with that wanker.

He followed Lunny into his office and dropped onto the single visitor's chair clear of paperwork, discarded uniform or fishing tackle.

The sergeant aligned and re-aligned a stack of files. Finally, he said, 'Well, you see. Oh, hell, mate. Kat's–'

'What's wrong with Kat?' Franklin straightened, alarmed.

'It's nothing like that. She's in a bit of strife–'

'Shit. What is it this time?'

'She and her two cronies took a five-finger discount at Coles.'

Franklin groaned, raking his sandy-coloured hair. The trio had received a day's suspension for smoking in the school toilets three weeks ago and he'd grounded his daughter for a month. He'd given her time off for good behaviour, and here she was, caught shoplifting days later.

'She's in Vinnie's office,' Lunny added, patting him awkwardly.

Franklin clamped his jaw, squashed on his cap and plucked keys for the marked four-wheel drive from the board.

The ninety-second drive felt protracted. And so did the walk of fucking humiliation from the truck through the car park to the innards of the supermarket. Never before had he been as conscious of the downside of living and working in such an intimate community. He knew scores of Daylesford's permanent residents after so long in town.

Tight-chested, Franklin pushed through the two-way door to the labyrinth of offices and storerooms.

He and Vinnie shook hands, then the store owner cut to the chase. 'Frankie, we don't need to take this further for a handful of Mars Bars.'

Franklin lifted his palms and let them drop.

'C'mon, the girls are pretty upset,' Vinnie coaxed, then frowned. '*Except* Narelle King. If it was her alone,' he mimed spitting, 'I'd tell you to throw the book.'

'I don't know–'

'Frankie, Frankie! Put the fear of God in them and then let it be. Go!'

Still undecided, Franklin thrust open Vinnie's door. He saw Kat flanked by her partners in crime on the sofa. While she glared, Lisa turned grey-white and Narelle reclined, blasé.

'You two.' Franklin jerked his head at Lisa and Narelle. 'Out.'

When they'd gone, he used his daughter's formal name. 'Katrina. What happened?'

She scowled harder.

He waited.

Kat clasped a hunk of her long hair. She twirled crimped blonde strands in front of her face, looking through him with clones of his own eyes. While biased and blind to their many similarities, Franklin considered her a stunner. But she was ugly with insolence now.

He faced away and leaned on Vinnie's desk. He counted to ten, then twenty. When he turned, his daughter hadn't budged.

'What am I doing wrong?'

Parents had to shoulder some blame. It ate him up to realise he'd failed her somehow.

She eye-rolled.

'Smoking, now this. What next?'

Franklin hated to see Kat make mistakes. Her next rebellious act could end in heartbreak.

She sniffed.

'I've got nothing to say to you.' The utter disappointment in his voice made her flinch.

Finally, a reaction.

Franklin pulled open the door. Narelle stumbled, caught eavesdropping.

'We're going to the station.'

The instant Kat brought Narelle King home, Franklin had identified her as a brazen troublemaker. It wasn't her bottle-blonde hair, bazooka boobs or that she carried a street-savvy sophistication from living in Melbourne until she was thirteen. Pure and simple, she'd failed Franklin's attitude test then and perpetually since. Even so, he recognised the futility of forbidding Kat's friendship with King. You don't give your teenage daughter yet another reason for defiance.

He seized the scruff of King's neck and pushed her forward. Lisa Cantrell snuffled as she trudged in the rear. Franklin sympathised with her. Studious and timid, she was an odd fit with the other two.

Franklin shepherded the girls to the truck, feeling as miserable as Lisa. His aim was to let them imagine the worst possible outcome, while he tried not to think about local gossipmongers. He hid behind dark sunglasses and the peak of his police cap and zipped through the roundabout and two blocks to the station.

Slumped on the stool next to Matty, Georgie chomped peanuts and surveyed her companion in the mirror. His face was animated. Everyone else in this bar appeared happy too. It only made her crappy mood spiral further.

Outside was the same story. The brief shower had ceased. The road steamed warm air. After five on a Friday afternoon, the working week surrendered to the weekend. Men ripped off ties and undid top buttons. Women greeted friends as if they hadn't seen them for a month. There was saccharine sweetness all around but for her.

She slugged beer. Then the brew curdled.

Fight or flight?

Why not both?

Take time out from my messed-up life while I do a favour for Ruby. That works for me.

'I'm outta here.' Georgie slammed down her Corona, spilling it onto the stainless top.

'Need a lift, Gee?'

'Nuh, ta, I've got the Spider. Besides, you're not going anywhere near where I'm headed.'

'Where's that?'

'Daylesford.'

Before he could ask why, she hoisted handbag and court file, pecked his cheek and threaded her way to the exit.

'Gee!'

Surprised, she spun around. Half the pub froze.

'Should you be driving?' Matty pointed to the abandoned beer.

'I'll take my chances,' Georgie said, then mustered what

dignity she could and merged into the commuter exodus on William Street.

We hope you enjoyed the opening of *Tell Me Why* and would like to read more. *Black Cloud* is the latest and fourth instalment in the Georgie Harvey and John Franklin series.

Dear reader,

We hope you enjoyed reading *On The Job*. Please take a moment to leave a review, even if it's a short one. Your opinion is important to us.

Discover more books by Sandi Wallace at https://www.nextchapter.pub/authors/sandi-wallace

Want to know when one of our books is free or discounted for Kindle? Join the newsletter at http://eepurl.com/bqqB3H

Best regards,

Sandi Wallace and the Next Chapter Team

More of Sandi Wallace's short crime stories are in:

Murder in the Midst

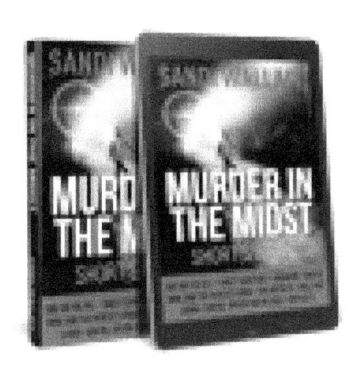

For your copy, please head to:

http://mybook.to/murdermidst

ACKNOWLEDGMENTS

My love of crime fiction began at a very early age, thanks to a steady diet of mystery and adventure stories, as did my dream of becoming a crime writer. But if the pull to be an author hadn't been so strong, I fancy I would have been a police detective.

When I left school, I failed the Victoria Police height requirement, which was later abolished. After that, I came close to joining up a few times, but ultimately chose to fight and solve crime from behind my computer instead. It was the right choice. But that doesn't mean my interest in policing has diminished.

This is my first short-fiction collection and each story features police characters. Some of these short stories are award-winners and have been previously published. Others are new and never-before-released tales, including 'The Job' parts I to VI, a series of verse shadowing the careers of fresh-faced uniformed officers, seasoned detectives, and old coppers on the brink of retirement, and each part links with what follows in the next short story.

Any mistakes are my own. But I give thanks to the police members who assisted with my procedural questions: David

Spencer, then attached to Victoria Police Media & Corporate Communications Department, Film and Television Office, and Tessa Jenkins and Joanne Morrison. Special mentions are also extended to Ruth Kennedy, Marianne Vincent, Lana Pecherczyk, Ebony McKenna, Judy Elliot, Raylea O'Loughlin, Sharon Gurry, Michelle Somers, and Rowena Holloway.

My sincere thanks too, of course, to the team at Next Chapter.

There are many others who inspire, encourage, and support me, but none more than you, my readers. Thank you. You keep me writing and sharing, and I'd love you to join me on Facebook and Instagram or follow my website.

And last, but never least, cheers to Glenn, for always believing in me.

ABOUT THE AUTHOR

Sandi Wallace's crime-writing apprenticeship comprised devouring as many crime stories as possible, developing her interest in policing, and working stints as banker, paralegal, cabinetmaker, office manager, executive assistant, personal trainer and journalist. She has won a host of prizes for her short crime fiction including several Scarlet Stiletto Awards and her debut novel *Tell Me Why* won the Davitt Award Readers' Choice. Sandi is currently at work on a psychological thriller. She is still an avid reader of crime and loves life in the Dandenong Ranges outside of Melbourne with her husband.

Connect with Sandi at

Website www.sandiwallace.com
Amazon www.amazon.com/author/sandiwallace
Goodreads www.goodreads.com/author/show/
8431978.Sandi_Wallace
Facebook www.facebook.com/sandi.wallace.crimewriter
Instagram www.instagram.com/sandiwallacecrime
Pinterest www.pinterest.com.au/sandiwallace_crimewriter/

Lightning Source UK Ltd.
Milton Keynes UK
UKHW021845071220
374768UK00011B/944/J